Jane A
Sense and Sensibility

Adapted by Jen Taylor
with Book-It Repertory Theatre

A SAMUEL FRENCH ACTING EDITION

FOUNDED 1830

SAMUELFRENCH.COM
SAMUELFRENCH-LONDON.CO.UK

FOR PRODUCTION ENQUIRIES

UNITED STATES AND CANADA
Info@SamuelFrench.com
1-866-598-8449

UNITED KINGDOM AND EUROPE
Plays@SamuelFrench-London.co.uk
020-7255-4302

Each title is subject to availability from Samuel French, depending upon country of performance. Please be aware that *SENSE AND SENSIBILITY* may not be licensed by Samuel French in your territory. Professional and amateur producers should contact the nearest Samuel French office or licensing partner to verify availability.

MUSIC USE NOTE

Licensees are solely responsible for obtaining formal written permission from copyright owners to use copyrighted music in the performance of this play and are strongly cautioned to do so. If no such permission is obtained by the licensee, then the licensee must use only original music that the licensee owns and controls. Licensees are solely responsible and liable for all music clearances and shall indemnify the copyright owners of the play(s) and their licensing agent, Samuel French, against any costs, expenses, losses and liabilities arising from the use of music by licensees. Please contact the appropriate music licensing authority in your territory for the rights to any incidental music.

IMPORTANT BILLING AND CREDIT REQUIREMENTS

If you have obtained performance rights to this title, please refer to your licensing agreement for important billing and credit requirements.

SENSE AND SENSIBILITY was first commissioned, developed and produced in the Book-It Style® by Book-It Repertory Theatre (Jane Jones and Myra Platt, founding co-artistic directors; Charlotte Tiencken, managing director) in Seattle, Washington on June 3, 2011. The performance was directed by Makaela Pollock, with sets by Pete Rush, costumes by Deane Middleton, lights by Amiya Brown, sound by Kevin Heard, props by Clare Strasser, and choreography by Laura Ferri. The Production Stage Manager was Kristyne Hughes. The cast was as follows:

ELINOR DASHWOOD	Kjerstine Anderson
MARIANNE DASHWOOD	Jessica Martin
MARGARET DASHWOOD/MISS GREY	Samantha Leeds
MRS DASHWOOD	Amy Fleetwood
HENRY DASHWOOD/SIR JOHN MIDDLETON/ APOTHECARY	Bill Johns
JOHN DASHWOOD/MR. PALMER	Shawn Law
FANNY DASHWOOD/CHARLOTTE PALMER	Emily Grogan
EDWARD AND ROBERT FERRARS	Jason Marr
MRS JENNINGS	Karen Nelsen
COLONEL BRANDON	David Quicksall
JOHN WILLOUGHBY	Aaron Blakely
LUCY STEELE	Angela DiMarco
THOMAS/SERVANT	Jacob Breslauer
SERVANT	Sarah Warren

CHARACTERS

ELINOR DASHWOOD (late teens/early 20s)

MARIANNE DASHWOOD (late teens)

MARGARET DASHWOOD (early teens)

MRS DASHWOOD (40s)

HENRY DASHWOOD (50's)

JOHN DASHWOOD (mid to late 20s)

FANNY DASHWOOD (mid 20s)

EDWARD FERRARS (mid 20s)

SIR JOHN MIDDLETON (40's)

MRS JENNINGS (50's)

COLONEL BRANDON (late 30s)

JOHN WILLOUGHBY (mid 20s)

CHARLOTTE PALMER (20's)

MR. PALMER (late 20s)

LUCY STEELE (early 20s)

ROBERT FERRARS (early 20s)

THOMAS

SERVANTS

MISS GREY

APOTHECARY

SETTING

England 1811

NOTES ON THE TEXT

Overlapping lines – // in a line indicates the point that the next line begins.

Bows/Curtsies – This is similar to a formal handshake used at every meeting and goodbye.

Lucy Steele's grammatical errors are just that. Please don't "correct" them.

Any scene changes should be swift and fluid and occur under dialogue as much as possible. Unnecessary blackouts and transitions between scenes will stall the dramatic momentum of the play.

Set should be simple and suggestive to support seamless scene changes. Allow lighting and barest of set pieces and props to serve the storytelling. For example, the pianoforte may easily be indicated with a chair and mime without using an actual instrument.

IMPORTANT NOTE ON THE BOOK-IT STYLE ®

The use of narrative, particularly third-person narrative, is a hallmark and founding principle of Book-It Repertory Theatre productions since the company's founding in 1990. Book-It's approach to narrative text on stage is known throughout theatre communities regionally and nationally as the "Book-It Style®." Book-It adaptations provide an experience of the book unlike other stage adaptations. By preserving the author's original language, Book-It adaptations capture the essence of the novel's original intent and tone, while celebrating the author's unique voice.

Actors in a Book-It Style production perform narrative lines in character with objectives and actions as they would with any line of dialogue in a standard play. Narrative lines are delivered with motivation to other characters, as opposed to a detached delivery straight out to the audience as a narrator. For example, in the excerpt below, the third-person narrative looks as though it is simple expository character description, but actually plays out as a spat between the two sisters and their mother, demonstrating their different temperaments and outlooks on life.

> (**ELINOR**, **MRS DASHWOOD** *and* **MARIANNE** *enter together into the drawing room.* **MARIANNE** *plays a very sad song on the pianoforte*)

MRS DASHWOOD. Oh, Marianne… not that song.

> (**MARIANNE** *stops playing then begins playing a different sad piece*)

ELINOR. *(asking* **MARIANNE** *for moderation)* Marianne was sensible and clever;

MARIANNE. yet eager in everything: her sorrows, her joys,

ELINOR. could have no moderation.

MRS DASHWOOD. She was generous, amiable, interesting! She was everything-

ELINOR. but prudent!

Book-It adapters will often divide descriptive narrative amongst several characters. This arrangement and editing process is a result of purposeful exploration and development over the last 28 years of the company's artistic history, and overseen by Founding Co-Artistic Directors Jane Jones and Myra Platt.

The director of a Book-It script must envision the narrative as a significant element to the production; designers are crucial in facilitating the process by providing simple and sensitive solutions keeping the staging fluid and the audience's imagination engaged. Embracing the use of narrative is the foundation of Book-It's scripts and serves to create a singular theatre experience for both theatre artist and theatregoer.

For more information on the Book-It Style, or to arrange for a master class for your cast or production company, please visit www.book-it.org or call (206)216-0877.

ACT I

Scene One

(Norland Park. Lights up on **ELINOR** *and* **MARIANNE DASHWOOD** *onstage full of energy.)*

ELINOR. The family of Dashwood…

MARIANNE. had been long settled in Sussex

ELINOR. At Norland Park.

MARIANNE. Dear dear Norland!

*(***HENRY*** and* **MRS DASHWOOD** *stroll onstage together.* **MARGARET** *follows. They all go about their activities in the drawing room; reading, playing music, etc. It is a lively, happy family.)*

HENRY. The present owner of the estate,

MRS DASHWOOD. Mr. Henry Dashwood,

HENRY. had three daughters, by his present lady

MRS DASHWOOD. *(Kissing their cheeks or handing them a book or a paintbrush, etc.)* Elinor, Marianne, …

HENRY. *(Offering a book to* **MARGARET.***)* and Margaret. Have you begun reading this, my child?

MARGARET. "Romeo and Juliet"? *(She nods.)*

HENRY. I look forward to our discussion at supper.
"But, soft! What light through yonder window breaks?
It is the east, and Juliet is the sun!"

MRS DASHWOOD. "Arise, fair sun, and kill the envious moon,"

HENRY. "Who is already sick and pale with grief,
That thou her maid art far more fair than she."

(The girls applaud.)

MRS DASHWOOD. Oh darling.

(**HENRY** *and* **MRS DASHWOOD** *stroll arm in arm.*
MARIANNE *plays a happy tune on the pianoforte.)*

ELINOR. Margaret—

MARGARET. *(Who has already forgotten about the book.) Oui, ma soeur,* Elinor.

ELINOR. *Très bon* Margaret. *Maintenant,* Shakespeare e*t pas plus français, ma petite.*

MARGARET. *Mais j'adore le français!*

ELINOR. *Oui, je sais—*

MARIANNE. *Nous savons. Tout le monde sait!*

(Light special on **JOHN DASHWOOD**.*)*

HENRY. *(Speaking to* **MRS DASHWOOD**.*)* Henry Dashwood also had one son by a former marriage.

JOHN. This son, Mr. John Dashwood, was amply provided for by the fortune of his mother, which had been large, and by his own marriage which had added greatly to his wealth.

MRS DASHWOOD. Henry Dashwood's *daughters,* had no such fortune awaiting them as *their* mother had nothing—

HENRY. and Henry, under the terms of his own inheritance, was unable to leave them more than a pittance. To Henry's son, John Dashwood, the entire estate was—

JOHN. Entailed!

MRS DASHWOOD. in such a way as to leave no power of providing for Henry's wife and daughters!

MARGARET. Entailed?

MRS DASHWOOD. By law, neither you, nor your sisters, nor I may inherit Norland from your father.

HENRY. *(Laughing.)* Do not worry, my love, I may reasonably hope to live many years.

MRS DASHWOOD. *(As* **HENRY** *sits.)* But a sudden, severe illness…

(**HENRY** *is unwell. The ladies go to his aid with blankets or water, etc. The chair becomes his deathbed. Light special out as* **JOHN** *now enters the scene.*)

MRS DASHWOOD. Henry's son was sent for as soon as the danger was known.

(**HENRY** *pulls* **JOHN** *close so the ladies do not hear.*)

HENRY. John, my son! John...you inherit everything. Your sisters and their mother... I tried...but they will have so little. Please John...do *everything* in your power. Provide for them...promise me...promise!

JOHN. Yes sir...yes, of course, I shall.

HENRY. Thank you my boy. You've always done right, my son... My dear son...

(**HENRY** *gently dies. The women are distraught.*)

Scene Two

(HENRY exits. During the following, all get into black clothing, or pieces of it. FANNY enters.)

JOHN. No sooner was his father's funeral over, than Mrs. John Dashwood,

FANNY. arrived!! with the intention of *taking over* the household of Norland Park! No one could dispute her right to come; the house was her husband's from the moment of his father's death;

(FANNY and JOHN are too busy examining the house to hear the following.)

MARIANNE. but the indelicacy of her conduct was so great!

MRS DASHWOOD. What of her sense of honor? Of generosity?

ELINOR. Fanny Dashwood had never been a favorite with any of her husband's family;

MARIANNE. as she was even *more* cold hearted, narrow-minded and selfish than her husband, John.

FANNY. She had had no opportunity till the present, however, of showing them with how little attention to the comfort of other people she could act when occasion required it.

JOHN. Mrs. John Dashwood now installed herself as mistress of Norland!

(FANNY and JOHN exit.)

MRS DASHWOOD. I am a *visitor* in my own home! The most ungracious behavior—we shall leave tomorrow. Pack everything tonight!

MARIANNE. Yes, we cannot stay here any longer with that woman!

ELINOR. And go where? With what money, Mama? Remember, we've merely five hundred pounds a year now. Had we not best pause and consider? Marianne, I am sure that Fanny does not mean to be rude.

MRS DASHWOOD. Oh!

ELINOR. Let us reflect tonight and reconsider in the morning. We cannot now, at this perilous time, lose the friendship and protection of our only brother. And the impropriety of our immediate removal would—

MRS DASHWOOD. Yes, dear Elinor, of course you are right.

ELINOR. To set your mind at ease, Mama, I shall begin looking for a new home.

Scene Three

(Ladies exit. Lights shift as **JOHN** *and* **FANNY** *enter in a different part of the house.)*

JOHN. I've decided to give my sisters a thousand pounds apiece!

FANNY. So generous, my dear. Such a very large sum to throw away to the Miss Dashwoods. The Miss *Dashwoods*, who are related only by half blood, which, you know, is really no relationship at all. You would ruin yourself with your own generosity.

JOHN. It was my father's last request to me that I should assist his widow and daughters.

FANNY. He was on his deathbed! I dare say; ten-to-one but he was light-headed at the time.

JOHN. He did not stipulate for any particular sum, my dear Fanny; he only requested me, in general terms, to assist them.

FANNY. Then consider, that when the money is once parted with, it never can return.

JOHN. Perhaps then, five hundred pounds apiece? That would be a prodigious increase to their fortunes!

FANNY. What brother on Earth would do half so much?

JOHN. I would not wish to do any thing cheap. One had rather, on such occasions, do too much than too little. No one, at least, can think I have not done enough for them.

FANNY. Of course not! Already, they will have *five hundred* a-year amongst them.

JOHN. That is very true, and, therefore, perhaps a hundred a year in annuity for their mother instead during her lifetime—

FANNY. To be sure, it is better than parting with fifteen hundred pounds at once. But then if Mrs. Dashwood should live fifteen years, we shall be completely taken in.

JOHN. Fifteen years?!

FANNY. People always live forever when there is any annuity to be paid them.

JOHN. How unpleasant. I believe you are right, my love. Certainly whatever I may give them *occasionally* will be of far greater assistance than a yearly allowance. A present of fifty pounds, now and then, will prevent their ever being distressed for money, and will, I think, be amply discharging my promise to my father.

FANNY. To be sure it will. Indeed, to say the truth, I am convinced that your father had no idea of your giving them any money at all. The assistance he thought of, I dare say, was helping them to move their things, and sending them presents of fish and game, and so forth. What on Earth can four women want for more than five hundred pounds a year? They will have no carriage, no horses, and hardly any servants; they will keep no company, and can have no expenses of any kind! Only conceive how comfortable they will be!

(JOHN *and* FANNY *exit.*)

Scene Four

> (ELINOR, MRS DASHWOOD, *and* MARIANNE
> *enter together into the drawing room.* MARIANNE
> *plays a very sad song on the pianoforte.*)

MRS DASHWOOD. Oh, Marianne...not that song.

> (MARIANNE *stops playing then begins playing a
> different sad piece.*)

ELINOR. *(Asking* MARIANNE *for moderation.)* Marianne was *sensible* and clever;

MARIANNE. yet eager in everything: her sorrows, her joys,

ELINOR. could have no moderation.

MRS DASHWOOD. She was generous, amiable, interesting! She was *everything—*

ELINOR. but prudent!

MARIANNE. *(She has stopped playing and is with her mother.)* The resemblance between Marianne and her mother was strikingly great.

MRS DASHWOOD. They encouraged each other now in the violence of their affliction.

MARIANNE. The agony of grief which overpowered them at first, was voluntarily renewed,

MRS DASHWOOD. was sought for,

MARIANNE. was created again and again.

MRS DASHWOOD. They gave themselves up wholly to their sorrow!

> (MARIANNE *and* MRS DASHWOOD *embrace,
> sobbing.*)

ELINOR. *(Attempting to comfort them.)* Elinor, too, was deeply afflicted; but still she could struggle, she could exert herself and strive to rouse her mother to similar exertion and encourage her sister to similar forbearance.

> (MRS DASHWOOD *and* MARIANNE *are beyond
> hearing* ELINOR.)

ELINOR. Margaret?!

> (**MARGARET** *enters.*)

MARGARET. was a good-humored girl. Of thirteen. *Oui,*
Elinor?

ELINOR. *Aidez – moi!*

MARGARET. *Comment est-ce que je peux t'aider?*

ELINOR. *Voila!*

> (**MARGARET** *goes to* **MARIANNE** *and* **MRS
> DASHWOOD**.)

MARGARET. Mama?

MRS DASHWOOD. Oh my darling child!

> (**MRS DASHWOOD** *embraces* **MARGARET** *who then
> dissolves into tears with them. They move upstage.*)

ELINOR. *Ah oui.*

> (*A ring at the door.* **FANNY** *and* **JOHN** *hurry
> onstage.* **SERVANT** *leads* **EDWARD FERRARS** *on.*)

SERVANT. Mr. Edward Ferrars.

FANNY. Finally! Edward, we've been waiting for weeks!

EDWARD. Weeks? I'm sorry Fanny, John. I felt it would be—
(Sees **ELINOR**.*)* Oh…

FANNY. This is my brother Mr. Edward Ferrars.
Miss Dashwood.

> *(Bow/curtsy.)*

EDWARD. My heartfelt condolences, Miss Dashwood. I'm
terribly sorry to intrude into your house of mourning.
I cannot imagine how…again, my deepest sympathies.

FANNY. Yes, yes but what took you so very long?

EDWARD. Ah, well our mother had many…errands to keep
me occupied.

FANNY. Ah!

> (*The recovered* **MRS DASHWOOD**, **MARGARET** *and*
> **MARIANNE** *step forward to be introduced.*)

FANNY. Mrs. Dashwood, my brother Mr. Edward Ferrars!

(The ladies silently bow/curtsy to **EDWARD** *as* **JOHN** *boasts to* **ELINOR** *down stage.)*

JOHN. Edward Ferrars is the eldest son of a man who had died VERY rich. Yes, he will come into a remarkable fortune, indeed. The whole of his inheritance, however, depends on the *inclination* of his mother.

*(***JOHN** *joins* **FANNY** *to show* **EDWARD** *the features of the house.* **MRS DASHWOOD** *and* **MARIANNE** *exit.)*

MARIANNE. *(Exiting.)* And now she brings her brother?!

MARGARET. Elinor, *vous devez m'aider maintenant.*

ELINOR. What is it Margaret?

MARGARET. *En français!*

ELINOR. Margaret.

*(***EDWARD** *overhears and moves to* **ELINOR** *and* **MARGARET.** **FANNY** *and* **JOHN** *continue to examine the house.)*

EDWARD. *Ah Mademoiselle Margaret, votre soeur est très...très occupèe, non? Peut-être, je rend service à...*um*...je peux vous...*goodness... *Mon français est...*terrible, // *n'est-ce pas?*

MARGARET. No //...*mais...*

ELINOR. No, no your French is...good, Mr. Ferrars. And thank you, I believe we can manage. You must be tired from your journey. Margaret, ring—

FANNY. Edward? Let me show you the house!

EDWARD. Excuse me.

*(***EDWARD,** **FANNY** *and* **JOHN** *walk upstage.* **MRS DASHWOOD** *re-enters with a letter.)*

MRS DASHWOOD. I've just had a response from the man at Dartmoor Abbey! It is being let!

ELINOR. Dartmoor *Abbey*? When did—Mama, Dartmoor Abbey is quite beyond our means.

MRS DASHWOOD. Oh Elinor, you would have us in Mr. Smith's shed!

*(**MRS DASHWOOD** and **MARGARET** exit.)*

ELINOR. *(Calling after them.)* The small *house* on Mr. Smith's property is perfectly suitable and within our means Mama. *(Beat.)* I will send out more enquiries.

*(**ELINOR** exits after them. **FANNY**, **EDWARD**, and **JOHN** move downstage.)*

FANNY. *(Conspiratorially.)* Yes, all the china, plate, *and* linen was left to Mrs. Dashwood and her *daughters*.

EDWARD. Well, I imagine being surrounded by things familiar will comfort—

FANNY. They are a great deal too handsome for any place THEY can ever afford to live in. But, however, so it is. Their father thought only of THEM. And the household! What disarray!

EDWARD. Fanny, they've just lost their father. Nothing will ever be the same for them.

*(**EDWARD** exits followed by **JOHN** and **FANNY**.)*

Scene Five

(It is a different day. **MARIANNE** *enters the drawing room and plays pianoforte.* **ELINOR** *then enters to paint. A moment.* **EDWARD** *enters.)*

EDWARD. Miss Dashwood. Miss Marianne.

*(***MARIANNE*** continues to play quietly.)*

ELINOR. Hello, Mr. Ferrars, did you enjoy your morning walk?

EDWARD. Oh yes! Norland's grounds are quite extensive. The old walnut trees are truly remarkable. *(Beat.)*

Unfortunately, I believe my sister has determined to build a greenhouse where they now reside.

ELINOR. *(Quietly.)* Oh. I hope Marianne does not learn that.

EDWARD. I'll do my part to keep it a secret.

ELINOR. Thank you. You've been here now many weeks. Are you enjoying Sussex, Mr. Ferrars?

EDWARD. Yes, indeed. As you know, I'm here at Fanny's request. She hopes to provide me something to do…*n'est-ce pas?*

ELINOR. *(Laughing.)* But, as a gentleman, you certainly have no occupation.

EDWARD. No, no…but my mother and sister—they long to see me distinguished.

ELINOR. As?

EDWARD. They hardly know. Some figure in the world! Politics, parliament or…driving a barouche! Would be enough.

ELINOR. And you?

EDWARD. I have no turn for barouches. *(They laugh.)* I'd prefer the church and a quiet life. But my younger brother, Robert, is more promising, fortunately.

ELINOR. Edward Ferrars was not recommended to their good opinion by any peculiar graces of person or address. His manners required intimacy to make them pleasing.

EDWARD. He was too diffident to do justice to himself;

(*EDWARD* shows **ELINOR** *a book which they share over the next few lines.* **MARIANNE** *has stopped playing and is now watching them.*)

ELINOR. but when his natural shyness was overcome, his behavior gave every indication of an open, affectionate heart.

EDWARD. His understanding was good, and his education

ELINOR. had given it solid improvement.

EDWARD. Miss Elinor Dashwood possessed a strength of understanding,

ELINOR. and coolness of judgment.

EDWARD. She had an excellent heart; her disposition was affectionate, and her feelings were strong;

ELINOR. but she knew how to govern them.

(*Awkward, intimate beat.*)

EDWARD. (*Recovering.*) You are quite a skilled artist, Miss Dashwood.

ELINOR. Thank you, Mr. Ferrars. It is my solace.

EDWARD. Yes, it is—it is very…

MARIANNE. (*Attempting to help*) Sylvan? …Bucolic? Verdant?

EDWARD. Green.

(**ELINOR** *laughs as does* **EDWARD.** **MARIANNE** *disappointedly moves away.*)

EDWARD. No, I quite like it. It reminds me of…but I've no knowledge of art. My studies didn't offer me that aspect of…indeed.

(**MRS DASHWOOD** *enters.* **EDWARD** *bows, exits.*)

MRS DASHWOOD. Edward. *He* is quiet and unobtrusive and does not disturb the wretchedness of my mind by ill-timed conversation. Have you heard any more news of a place for us, Elinor?

ELINOR. No, Mama, but I am determined to find us a suitable home. And yes—Edward… Edward could not be more different from his sister.

MRS DASHWOOD. Oh yes, yes, it is enough, to say that he is unlike Fanny is enough. It implies everything amiable. I love him already.

ELINOR. I think you will like him when you know more of him. You may *esteem* him.

Scene Six

(ELINOR *exits the drawing room and meets* EDWARD *upstage. They stroll together.*)

MRS DASHWOOD. Oh! ...Mrs. Dashwood *now* took pains to get acquainted with... Edward!

(*To* **MARIANNE**—*as they watch* ELINOR *and* EDWARD.) Edward is so pleasing and gentlemanlike. And even that quietness of manner— (*Waves it away.*) His heart is warm and his temper affectionate. He and Elinor are rarely apart these last few months...and have you perceived the way he looks at her? Soon, my dear Marianne. Elinor will, in all probability, be settled for life.

MARIANNE. Oh! Mama, how shall we do without her?

MRS DASHWOOD. My love, it will be scarcely a separation. We shall live within a few miles of each other and you will gain a brother, a *real* brother.

MARIANNE. Edward is...very amiable and I've grown to feel for him tenderly...but—yet—there is a something wanting. He has none of that grace which I should expect in the man who could seriously attach *my sister!* And I am afraid, Mama, he has no real taste. How spiritless was Edward's manner in reading to us last night! Such indifference, I could hardly keep my seat.

(EDWARD *suddenly in light special as scene shifts to a moment from last night.* ELINOR *watches him.*)

EDWARD. (*Reading awkwardly.*) "Wide o'er the brim, with many a torrent swell'd,

And the mix'd ruin of its banks o'erspread,

At last the rous'd-up river pours along;

Resistless, roaring, dreadful, down it comes

From the rude mountain, and the mossy wild,"

(*Light special out.* EDWARD *and* ELINOR *resume their walk.*)

MRS DASHWOOD. He would have done more justice to simple prose.

MARIANNE. Mama, if he is not to be animated by—

MRS DASHWOOD. We must allow for differences of taste.

MARIANNE. It would have broke *my* heart had I loved him! But Elinor has not my feelings and therefore she may overlook it and be happy with him. The more I know of the world, the more am I convinced that I shall never see a man whom I can really love. I require so much! He must have all Edward's *virtues*, and...

> *(Unable to verbalize,* **MARIANNE** *strikes a dramatic chord at the pianoforte.* **FANNY** *appears and whisks* **EDWARD** *off with her. He bows to* **ELINOR** *as he exits.)*

FANNY. Edward!

> *(***ELINOR** *re-enters the drawing room.)*

MRS DASHWOOD. Darlings. Excuse me.

> *(***MRS DASHWOOD** *exits.* **ELINOR** *returns to her painting.)*

MARIANNE. What a pity it is, Elinor, that Edward should have no taste for drawing.

ELINOR. No taste for drawing, why should you think so? He does not draw himself, indeed, but he has a great pleasure in seeing the performances of other people, and his discernment is by no means deficient.

MARIANNE. Marianne was afraid of offending and said no more on the subject.

ELINOR. I hope, Marianne you do not consider him as deficient in *general* taste.

MARIANNE. I have the highest opinion in the world of his goodness and sense. I think him every thing that is... worthy and amiable.

ELINOR. I do not perceive how you could express yourself more warmly. Of his sense and goodness no one can, I think, be in doubt. But, I have studied his sentiments and heard his opinions and, though his *shyness* often keeps him silent, I believe that his mind is well informed, his imagination lively and his *taste* delicate and pure. His abilities in every respect improve upon acquaintance...at first sight, his person can hardly be called handsome, till the expression of his eyes which are uncommonly good—

MARIANNE. I shall very soon think him handsome, Elinor, when you tell me to love him as a brother.

ELINOR. Elinor was sorry for the warmth she had been betrayed into, in speaking of him. I do not attempt to deny that I think very highly of him—that I greatly esteem—that I like him.

MARIANNE. Esteem him! Like him! Cold-hearted Elinor! Oh! worse than cold-hearted! Use those words again, and I will leave the room this moment.

ELINOR. *(Laughing.)* Believe my feelings to be stronger than I have declared; but farther than this you must not believe. I am by no means assured of his regard for me. In my heart I feel little – scarcely any doubt of his preference but...there are other considerations. Edward is very far from being financially independent and there would be many difficulties in his way if he were to wish to marry a woman who had not either a great fortune or high rank.

MARIANNE. You really are not engaged to him? Yet it certainly soon will happen!

   *(***MARIANNE*** exits.)*

ELINOR. Elinor could not consider her partiality for Edward in so prosperous a state as Marianne believed it. There was, at times, a want of spirits about him.

   *(***EDWARD*** enters, sees **ELINOR**, pauses, grabs a book, exits. **FANNY** quietly enters and sees this.)*

ELINOR. Nay, the longer she knew him, the more doubtful seemed the nature of his regard; and sometimes Elinor believed it to be no more than friendship.

(**ELINOR** *exits.* **MRS DASHWOOD** *enters, passing through the room.*)

FANNY. Edward is a remarkable young man!

MRS DASHWOOD. Indeed, Fanny…we are all delighted with Edward.

FANNY. He has great expectations, of course. Politics. Parliament. He shall marry very well. My mother has made sure both her sons shall…and any young woman who might attempt to *draw him in*…would be sorely disappointed.

MRS DASHWOOD. Mrs. Dashwood could neither pretend to be insensible, nor endeavor to be calm. I understand, indeed. Thank you Fanny!

(**MRS DASHWOOD** *begins to exit.* **ELINOR** *enters,* **FANNY** *gives her an opened letter and exits.*)

Scene Seven

ELINOR. *(Reading.)* Mama, we've an offer of a small house in Devonshire, and the rent is uncommonly moderate. It's farther from Norland than we'd hoped—

MRS DASHWOOD. *(Reading the letter.)* From my cousin, Sir John!

> *(**SIR JOHN** appears in a light special.)*

SIR JOHN. It is come to my attention that you, cousin, are in need of a dwelling; and though the house I have to offer is merely a cottage, I assure you that everything shall be done to it which you might think necessary. You and your lovely daughters! Do visit Barton *Cottage*, and judge whether it could be made comfortable to you.

MRS DASHWOOD. To escape my daughter-in-law! Such a blessing! Mrs. Dashwood instantly wrote Sir John Middleton her acknowledgment of his kindness, and her acceptance of his proposal.

> *(**SIR JOHN**'s special out as he exits. **JOHN**, **FANNY**, **EDWARD**, **MARIANNE**, **MARGARET**, and **THOMAS** enter preparing for the journey as **MARIANNE** soliloquizes.)*

MARIANNE. Dear, dear Norland! When shall I learn to feel a home elsewhere! Oh! happy house, could you know what I suffer in now viewing you from this spot! And you, ye well-known trees! No leaf will decay because we are removed. No, you will continue the same, insensible of any change in those who walk under your shade! But who will remain to enjoy you?

EDWARD. I hope you will not be settled far from Norland.

MRS DASHWOOD. We are settling in Devonshire.

EDWARD. Devonshire. Are you...? So far?

MRS DASHWOOD. It is but a cottage owned by my dear cousin, Sir John Middleton, but I hope to see many of my friends in it. // Mrs. Dashwood concluded with a very

EDWARD. Devonshire…

FANNY. *kind* invitation to John and Fanny to visit her at Barton;

MRS DASHWOOD. and to Edward, she gave one with still greater affection.

> (**FANNY** *and* **JOHN** *exit. Others prepare to leave.* **EDWARD** *and* **ELINOR** *stand apart from the family.*)

EDWARD. Well then… I understand your Servant, Thomas, is going with you to Barton?

ELINOR. Indeed, he is.

EDWARD. Good…good. *(Long silence.)* Miss Dashwood… these many months I've spent here with…

ELINOR. *(Beat.)* Yes…?

EDWARD. I hope… I've…*much* to…

> (**EDWARD** *and* **ELINOR** *simply look at one another for a long moment.*)

ELINOR. Goodbye, Mr. Ferrars. I shall miss—our conversations.

EDWARD. Indeed…goodbye, Miss Dashwood.

> (**EDWARD** *exits as the ladies and* **THOMAS** *begin their journey.*)

Scene Eight

(Transition. Travel to Barton.)

MRS DASHWOOD. The first part of their journey

ELINOR. was performed in too melancholy a disposition to be otherwise than unpleasant.

MARIANNE. But as they drew towards the end of it, their interest in the country and

MARGARET. the view!

MARIANNE. gave them cheerfulness.

MRS DASHWOOD. It was a pleasant, fertile spot.

(They've now arrived at Barton Cottage.)

ELINOR. As a house, Barton Cottage was comfortable and compact.

MARIANNE. As a cottage, it was defective, for the building was regular, the roof was tiled, the window shutters were not painted green, nor were the walls covered with honeysuckles. In comparison of Norland, Barton Cottage was poor, small and extremely isolated indeed.

THOMAS. The situation of the house was good.

MARGARET. High hills rose immediately behind and on each side.

THOMAS. and the prospect in front of the cottage commanded the whole of the valley!

ELINOR. They were all wise enough to be contented with the house as it was.

Scene Nine

(Transition to Barton Park. **SIR JOHN** *enters.* **THOMAS** *exits.)*

MRS DASHWOOD. The very next evening, their benefactor, Sir John Middleton, sent his carriage and the Dashwoods rode the few miles to his home in great comfort.

SIR JOHN. Welcome to Barton Park, fair Dashwoods! How was your journey? You are safe and sound I see. Wonderful!

MRS DASHWOOD. Sir John!

SIR JOHN. Mrs. Dashwood! I'm delighted.

MARIANNE. Sir John's home was large and handsome; hospitable and elegant.

SIR JOHN. You must be Miss Dashwood, Miss Marianne and Miss Margaret! Yes? I hope you are comfortably settled in your new home. Sadly, I have been unable to get any smart young men to join us tonight as...we've none for miles! *(Laughing at his own joke.)* My friend, Colonel Brandon will be here but he is neither very young nor very jovial. And my wife, Lady Middleton! You must meet my sweet wife...

(Sounds of children screaming offstage.)

CHILDREN. I want it!

Give me that!

Mummy said I could have it!

(Long scream of defiance.)

SIR JOHN. She is with the children, of course...absolutely devoted she is! But, luckily, my mother-in-law, Mrs. Jennings

*(***MRS JENNINGS*** enters as her name is said.)*

MRS JENNINGS. arrived at Barton within the last hour! Oh dear, my daughter is—

(Another scream from the children.)

SIR JOHN. *Occupied*, is she?

MRS JENNINGS. As always!

MRS DASHWOOD. Mrs. Jennings was a good-humored, merry woman,

MRS JENNINGS. who talked a great deal,

ELINOR. seemed very happy,

MARIANNE. and rather vulgar.

MRS JENNINGS. She was full of jokes!

MARGARET. and before dinner was over had said many *witty* things on the subject of lovers and husbands!

MRS JENNINGS. You beauties haven't left your hearts behind you in Sussex, have you? Oh! Miss Dashwood! I think you are blushing! What is his name?

SIR JOHN. Look out fair Dashwoods! My mother-in-law married off both of her daughters and now has nothing to do but to marry all the world!

> (**MRS JENNINGS** *and* **SIR JOHN** *dissolve into laughter.* **BRANDON** *enters.*)

Oh ladies! My friend, Colonel Brandon! The Dashwoods!

> (*Bows/curtsies.*)

BRANDON. Colonel Brandon

MRS DASHWOOD. was silent and grave. His appearance was not unpleasing—

MARIANNE. but he was on the *wrong* side of five and thirty.

BRANDON. His address was particularly

ELINOR. gentlemanlike.

MRS JENNINGS. I will not give up Miss Dashwood! I will discover the name of your love if it—ooh Miss Margaret, I see you smiling!

MARGARET. I must not tell, may I, Elinor?

MRS JENNINGS. OH! I was certain!

> (**SIR JOHN** *and* **MRS JENNINGS** *giggle delightedly.*)

ELINOR. Elinor tried to laugh too but the effort was painful.

MARIANNE. Margaret! Remember that whatever your conjectures may be, you have no right to repeat them.

MARGARET. Conjectures? It was you who told me of it yourself.

(**SIR JOHN** *and* **MRS JENNINGS** *laugh uproariously.*)

MRS JENNINGS. Oh! pray, Miss Margaret, let us know all about it. What is the gentleman's name? He is the curate of the parish at Norland I dare say.

MARGARET. No, *that* he is not. He is of no profession at all.

SIR JOHN. Oh! A gentleman!

MARIANNE. Margaret, you know that all this is an invention of your own, and that there is no such person in existence.

MARGARET. Well then he is lately dead, Marianne, for I am sure there was such a man once...and his name begins with an F.

MRS JENNINGS. I knew it! An F! An F! Fitzgerald! Franklin! Frederick!

(**MARIANNE** *quickly crosses to the piano and begins playing to distract.*)

Oh, goodness...well, oh dear. Delightful!

(**MARIANNE** *is very talented.*)

SIR JOHN. *(While she is playing.)* Remarkable! Just remarkable!

MRS JENNINGS. Oh yes! Bravo!

BRANDON. *(Quietly taken with* **MARIANNE.***)* Colonel Brandon alone heard her play without being in raptures. He paid Marianne only the compliment of attention;

(**MARIANNE** *finishes her song. All applaud and then the* **DASHWOODS** *prepare to leave.*)

MRS JENNINGS. *(To* **SIR JOHN**.*)* Mrs. Jennings was remarkably quick in the discovery of attachments. Mark my words, Colonel Brandon is very much in love with Marianne Dashwood!

SIR JOHN. Miss Marianne?

MRS JENNINGS. It would be an excellent match, for HE is rich—with his two thousand a year! —and SHE is handsome!

> (**DASHWOODS** *overhear this and then they are gone.* **MRS JENNINGS** *and* **SIR JOHN** *exit laughing.* **BRANDON** *follows them.*)

Scene Ten

*(Transition to Barton Cottage. **DASHWOODS** explode onto the stage, reading, painting, etc.)*

MARIANNE. Incomprehensible! I do not understand Mrs. Jennings! It is impertinent. It is absurd. Colonel Brandon is old enough to be my father; and if he were ever *animated* enough to be in love, he must have long outlived every sensation of the kind. When is a man to be safe from such wit, if age and infirmity will not protect him?

ELINOR. Infirmity!

MRS DASHWOOD. Oh yes, he is ancient.

ELINOR. You can hardly deceive yourself as to Colonel Brandon's having the use of his limbs!

MARIANNE. Did not you hear him complain of the rheumatism?

ELINOR. *(Amused.)* He merely chanced to complain of a slight rheumatic feel in one of his shoulders.

*(**ELINOR** exits.)*

MARIANNE. Mama, I am sure Edward Ferrars is not well. We have now been here almost a fortnight, and yet he does not come.

MRS DASHWOOD. Had you any idea of his coming so soon? I had none. Does Elinor expect him already?

MARIANNE. Of course, she must! How strange this is. Their behavior is unaccountable! How cold, how composed were her and Edward's last *adieus* at Norland! I don't understand it. When is Elinor dejected or melancholy? When does she try to avoid society, or appear restless and dissatisfied in it?

MRS DASHWOOD. Oh Marianne, Elinor is…not like us.

MARGARET. *(At the window.)* It has stopped raining! *C'ést fantastique!*

MRS DASHWOOD. *(Hinting.)* The whole country about them abounded in beautiful *walks*.

Scene Eleven

(Transition. On the Hills. **MRS DASHWOOD** *exits.)*

MARIANNE. I can see patches of blue sky, Margaret. Hurry!

MARGARET. The girls gaily ascended the downs!

MARIANNE. Is there a felicity in the world superior to this?

MARGARET. They pursued their way against the wind,

MARIANNE. when suddenly the clouds united over their heads, and a driving rain set full in their face.

MARGARET. They were obliged, though unwillingly, to turn back.

BOTH GIRLS. One consolation remained

MARIANNE. Racing, with all possible speed, down the steep side of a hill!

> *(The* **GIRLS** *race.* **MARIANNE** *falls, attempts to stand but cannot.)*

MARGARET. What is it, Marianne?

MARIANNE. A turned ankle is all…run and tell Mama!

> **(JOHN WILLOUGHBY,** *dressed in hunting gear, appears.)*

WILLOUGHBY. You are hurt. May I be of assistance?

MARIANNE. It's… I…

MARGARET. The gentleman took her up in his arms and carried her down the hill—

> **(WILLOUGHBY** *carries* **MARIANNE** *back to Barton Cottage.* **MARGARET** *follows.* **MRS DASHWOOD** *and* **ELINOR** *enter.)*

MRS DASHWOOD. directly into the house!

WILLOUGHBY. *(Placing* **MARIANNE** *gently upon a chaise.)* He apologized for his intrusion by relating its cause,

ELINOR. in a manner so frank and so graceful that his person,

MRS DASHWOOD. which was uncommonly handsome,

MARIANNE. received additional charms from his voice and expression.

MRS DASHWOOD. Thank you so very much, sir! Please, please be seated. We shall ring for tea... Elinor?

WILLOUGHBY. Thank you, Ma'am, I must decline as I am wet through and muddy as well. I hope, however, that I might have the honor of calling tomorrow to enquire after you? Miss...?

MRS DASHWOOD.	**MARIANNE.**
Marianne Dashwood	Marianne

MRS DASHWOOD. And to whom are *we* obliged, sir?

WILLOUGHBY. Willoughby. John Willoughby of Allenham. Excuse me and...good day.

> (**WILLOUGHBY** *exits with a bow.*)

MRS DASHWOOD. (*Enchanted.*) He then departed,

ELINOR. to make himself still more interesting,

MARIANNE. (*Enthralled.*) in the midst of a heavy rain.

MARGARET. That was... (*Words escape her, thus she giggles.*)

> (*All the* **DASHWOODS,** *excluding* **ELINOR**, *sigh in romantic reverie.*)

Scene Twelve

(Still at Barton Cottage. **SIR JOHN** *and* **BRANDON** *enter with flowers.)*

SIR JOHN. The next morning!

BRANDON. Sir John and Colonel Brandon called on them.

(Bows/Curtsies. **BRANDON** *gives flowers to* **MARIANNE.** *)*

BRANDON. I hope you are feeling better, Miss Marianne.

MARIANNE. Oh, thank you.

MRS DASHWOOD. How very kind, Colonel Brandon.

ELINOR. Do you know of any gentleman of the name of Willoughby at Allenham?

SIR JOHN. Willoughby! What, is he in the country? That is good news. I will ride over tomorrow, and ask him to dinner on Thursday.

MRS DASHWOOD. You know him then?

SIR JOHN. Know him! To be sure I do. Why, he is down here every year.

MRS DASHWOOD. And what sort of a young man is he?

SIR JOHN. As good a kind of fellow as ever lived, I assure you. A very decent shot!

MARIANNE. ...And is that all you can say for him? But what are his manners? What his pursuits, his talents, and genius?

SIR JOHN. Upon my soul, he is...a good humoured fellow, and...has got the nicest little black pointer I ever saw, eh Brandon? Was she out with him?

ELINOR. But who is he? Where does he come from? Has he a house at Allenham?

SIR JOHN. Oh! No, he has none of his own property here. He resides here only when he visits his elderly aunt at Allenham Court—which he will inherit upon her death. *His* estate is called Combe Magna in Somersetshire I believe. Yes, yes, he is very well worth catching I can tell you, Miss Dashwood! If I were you, I would not give him up to my younger sister, in spite of all this tumbling down hills. *(Laughing.)* Miss Marianne must not expect to have all the men to herself.

MRS DASHWOOD. I do not believe that Mr. Willoughby will be incommoded by the attempts of either of my daughters towards what you call *catching* him. It is not an employment to which they have been brought up. Men are very safe with us, let them be ever so rich. *(Beat.)* I am very glad to find, however, that he is a respectable young man.

> (**BRANDON** *and* **SIR JOHN** *ready themselves to leave, bowing, etc.*)

SIR JOHN. Well yes, he is as good a sort of fellow, I believe, as ever lived…and there is not a bolder rider in England.

> (**BRANDON** *leaves slightly ahead of* **SIR JOHN** *so as not to hear the following.*)

Aye, I see how it will be. Poor Brandon! he is quite smitten already.

> (**SIR JOHN** *exits as* **WILLOUGHBY** *enters.*)

(In passing.) Ah, Willoughby! Supper Thursday?

Scene Thirteen

MARIANNE. Marianne's preserver

WILLOUGHBY. soon called to make his personal enquiries.

MRS DASHWOOD. Oh, Mr. Willoughby, how delightful to see you! I must thank you again for your extraordinary kindness—your gallantry.

WILLOUGHBY. It was my honor, Mrs. Dashwood. And how are you feeling today, Miss Marianne?

MARIANNE. Better...much better, thank you! Marianne soon saw

WILLOUGHBY. that to the perfect good breeding of the gentleman,

MARIANNE. Willoughby united frankness and vivacity.

WILLOUGHBY. Of course I am passionately fond of music and dancing!

MARIANNE. Their taste was strikingly alike.

WILLOUGHBY. The same books—

MARIANNE. the same passages—

WILLOUGHBY & MARIANNE. were idolized by each.

MARIANNE. If any difference appeared it lasted no longer than till the force of Marianne's arguments

WILLOUGHBY. and the brightness of her eyes could be displayed. Willoughby acquiesced in all Marianne's decisions,

MARIANNE. caught all her enthusiasm;

WILLOUGHBY. and long before his visit concluded,

MARIANNE. Marianne and Willoughby conversed with the familiarity of a long-established—

WILLOUGHBY. friendship.

> (**WILLOUGHBY** *presents* **MARIANNE** *with a book, bows, exits.*)

ELINOR. Well, Marianne, for ONE morning I think you have done pretty well. You have already ascertained Mr. Willoughby's opinion in almost every matter of importance. Another meeting will suffice to explain his sentiments on picturesque beauty and second marriages, and then you can have nothing further to ask—

MARIANNE. Is this fair? Are my ideas so scanty? Oh I see what you mean. I have been too much at my ease, too happy, too frank. I have erred against every commonplace notion of decorum; I have been open and sincere where I ought to have been reserved, spiritless, dull, and deceitful.

MRS DASHWOOD. My love, do not be offended. Elinor was only in jest.

(**WILLOUGHBY** *re-enters.*)

WILLOUGHBY. Willoughby came to visit every day after this. To enquire after Marianne's health was at first his excuse;

ELINOR. but the encouragement of his reception made such an excuse unnecessary long before Marianne's perfect recovery.

(**MARIANNE** *stands and walks to* **WILLOUGHBY**.)

MRS DASHWOOD. Willoughby was a young man of good abilities,

MARIANNE. lively spirits, quick imagination and open, affectionate manners.

ELINOR. He was exactly formed to engage Marianne's heart.

WILLOUGHBY. His society

MARIANNE. became gradually her most exquisite enjoyment.

WILLOUGHBY. They read—

MARIANNE. they talked—

WILLOUGHBY. they sang together!

MARIANNE. (*Reading aloud.*) "An hour with thee! When earliest day

Dapples with gold the eastern gray,

Oh, what can frame my mind to bear
The toil and turmoil, cark and care,
// New griefs, which coming hours unfold,"

WILLOUGHBY. *(Without looking at the book.)* "New griefs, which coming hours unfold,
And sad remembrance of the old?
One hour with thee.

One hour with thee! When burning June
Waves his red flag at pitch of noon;
What shall repay the faithful swain,
His labor on the sultry plain;
And, more than cave or sheltering bough,
Cool feverish blood and throbbing brow?
One hour with thee."

   (Applause.)

MRS DASHWOOD. In Mrs. Dashwood's estimation he was as faultless as in Marianne's!

ELINOR. Elinor saw nothing to censure in Willoughby but a propensity of hastily forming and *giving* his opinion of other people, of saying *too* much what he thought.

WILLOUGHBY. Colonel Brandon is just the kind of man whom everybody speaks well of, and nobody cares about; whom all are delighted to see, and nobody remembers to talk to.

ELINOR. I like Colonel Brandon very much! Why should you dislike him?

WILLOUGHBY. I do not dislike him. I consider him, on the contrary, as a very respectable man, who has everybody's good word, and nobody's notice.

   (MARIANNE laughs.)

ELINOR. Colonel Brandon is sensible, well-informed, and good natured and I believe—

WILLOUGHBY. Miss Dashwood! You are endeavoring to disarm me by reason. But it will not do. I have three unanswerable reasons for disliking Colonel Brandon;

he threatened me with rain when I wanted it to be fine; he has found fault with the hanging of my carriage, and I cannot persuade him to buy my brown mare.

(**WILLOUGHBY** *and* **MARIANNE** *laugh together.*)

Scene Fourteen

(Transition to party at Barton Park.)

MRS DASHWOOD. Little had Mrs. Dashwood or her daughters imagined when they first came to this *isolated* part of the country

MARGARET. that so many engagements—such frequent invitations

MARIANNE. and such constant visitors would arise to occupy their time.

> *(**SIR JOHN, BRANDON, MRS JENNINGS,** and party guests enter.)*

SIR JOHN. Sir John threw private balls and dinner parties at least twice a week!

MARIANNE. In every meeting of the kind Willoughby was included!

ELINOR. Elinor could not be surprised at Marianne and Willoughby's attachment. She only wished that it were less openly shown.

> *(**BRANDON** steps forward to greet them and is ignored by **MARIANNE.**)*

WILLOUGHBY. When he was present

ELINOR. Marianne had no eyes for any one else.

MARIANNE. Marianne abhorred all concealment where no real disgrace could attend.

WILLOUGHBY. Everything Willoughby did

MARIANNE. was right.

WILLOUGHBY. Everything he said

MARIANNE. was clever.

ELINOR. This was the season of happiness to Marianne.

MARIANNE. Her heart was devoted to Willoughby.

SIR JOHN. Why don't you have a dance?

> *(All prepare to dance except **BRANDON** and **ELINOR.**)*

ELINOR. Elinor's happiness was not so great. Her heart was not so much at ease. Their amusements afforded her nothing to make amends for what she had left behind nor to teach her to think of Norland...and Edward with less regret than ever.

>   (**BRANDON** *crosses to* **ELINOR.**)

In Colonel Brandon alone, of all her new acquaintance, did Elinor find a person who could in any degree claim the respect of abilities,

BRANDON. excite the interest of friendship?

ELINOR. or give pleasure as a companion.

>   (**MARIANNE, WILLOUGHBY** *and others dance in*
>   *background.*)

BRANDON. I couldn't help overhearing your sister, Miss Marianne, declare her disbelief in *second* attachments.

ELINOR. Yes, her opinions are all romantic.

BRANDON. I see, so she considers them impossible to exist?

ELINOR. I believe she does. But how she contrives it without reflecting on the character of her own father, who had himself two wives, I know not. A few years, however, will settle her opinions more reasonably.

BRANDON. There is something so amiable in the prejudices of a young mind, that one is sorry to see them give way to the reception of more general opinions.

ELINOR. I cannot agree with you there. There are inconveniences attending such feelings as Marianne's. She sets propriety at nought; and a better acquaintance with the world is what I look forward to as her greatest possible advantage.

BRANDON. No, no, do not desire it. I once knew a lady who in temper and mind greatly resembled your sister, who thought and judged like her, but who from an enforced change—from a series of unfortunate circumstances...

>   (*Applause and chatter as dance ends.*)

SIR JOHN. Brandon!

BRANDON. Excuse me

(**BRANDON** *bows and crosses to* **SIR JOHN**.)

ELINOR. Elinor's compassion for Colonel Brandon now *increased*, as she had reason to suspect that the misery of disappointed love had *already* been known to him.

(**MRS JENNINGS** *steps forward*.)

MRS JENNINGS. Oh, is it now to be Colonel Brandon? Have you abandoned "Mr. F"? *(Laughing.)* Ah no, the Colonel... Alas, poor man, he is smitten elsewhere, isn't he? Alright, Miss Dashwood... Fairfax? Fieldman? Fairweather?

(**MARIANNE** *sends* **MARGARET** *over to distract*.)

MARGARET. Sir John just told the funniest joke, Mrs. Jennings.

MRS JENNINGS. Oh yes? Was it about Faithful Friends?!

(**MRS JENNINGS** *dissolves into laughter*. **MARGARET** *leads* **MRS JENNINGS** *away to* **SIR JOHN**.)

MARIANNE. Will Mrs. Jennings never tire of "Mr. F"?! But you will never believe *my* good news! Willoughby has given me a horse! Imagine, my dear Elinor, the delight of a gallop on some of these downs.

ELINOR. Oh, that *is* a delightful thought but... Marianne we've no stable for a horse, nor no servant to tend it or ride it. We can barely afford—

MARIANNE. Oh the expense would be a trifle!

ELINOR. Is it proper, Marianne, you accepting such a gift from a man of whom, though we admire, we know so little—

MARIANNE. You are mistaken, Elinor, in supposing I know but little of Willoughby. I am much better acquainted with him, than I am with most other creatures in the world. It is not time or opportunity that is to determine intimacy; it is disposition alone. Seven years would be insufficient to make some people acquainted with each other, and seven days are more than enough for others.

ELINOR. Elinor thought it wisest to touch that point no more. Only by an appeal to Marianne's affection for their mother and by representing the inconveniences and expense which that indulgent mother would surely have to draw on *herself—*

MARIANNE. was Marianne shortly subdued. She promised to tell Willoughby

> (**WILLOUGHBY** *approaches.*)

that the horse must be declined.

WILLOUGHBY. Marianne, the horse is still yours, though you cannot use it now. When you leave Barton to... form your own establishment, Queen Mab shall receive you!

> (**MARIANNE** *and* **WILLOUGHBY** *stroll away together.* **MRS DASHWOOD** *steps in to* **ELINOR.**)

MRS DASHWOOD. Mrs. Dashwood perceived an intimacy so decided, a meaning so direct, as marked a perfect agreement between them. He used her Christian name! They are engaged!

> (**MRS DASHWOOD** *turns back to the party.* **MARGARET** *now grabs* **ELINOR**'s *attention.*)

MARGARET. Oh, Elinor I have such a secret to tell you. I am sure Marianne will be married to Mr. Willoughby very soon for he has got a lock of her hair!

ELINOR. Take care, Margaret...

MARGARET. But, indeed, Elinor, I saw them! Last night after tea, when you and Mama went out of the room, he begged something of her, and then he took up her scissors and cut off a long lock of her hair! And then, he kissed it! I knew it! They are engaged!

Scene Fifteen

(Transition. Out of party to Barton Park's grounds. Preparing for an Outing.)

BRANDON. The following morning, a complete party of pleasure was to be enjoyed!

MARGARET. An adventure!

MRS JENNINGS. Colonel Brandon's grounds at Delaford are delightful.

MARGARET. I love an adventure!

SIR JOHN. Delaford is one of the most beautiful parks in the county!

BRANDON. With a large lake for sailing only twelve miles from Barton.

MRS JENNINGS. It is a bold undertaking, considering the time of year!

MRS DASHWOOD. However, the morning was rather favorable.

MARIANNE. They were all in high spirits!

*(A **SERVANT** enters with a letter for **BRANDON**.)*

SIR JOHN. Brandon, what is the matter?

MRS JENNINGS. No bad news, Colonel, I hope.

BRANDON. *(Clearly shaken.)* None at all, ma'am, I thank you. This letter, however, requires my immediate attendance in London.

MRS JENNINGS. In town!

BRANDON. Yes, but I am the more concerned, as I fear my presence is necessary to gain your admittance at Delaford.

*(**SERVANT** helps prepare **BRANDON** to depart.)*

SIR JOHN. You cannot go to London till tomorrow, Brandon, that is all.

BRANDON. It is not in my power to delay my journey for one day.

WILLOUGHBY. You would not be six hours later if you were to defer your journey till our return.

BRANDON. I cannot afford to lose one hour. My sincerest apologies!

(BRANDON hastily exits, SERVANT follows.)

WILLOUGHBY. *(To MARIANNE.)* There are some people who cannot bear a party of pleasure.

MRS JENNINGS. *(To ELINOR.)* Well, I can guess what his business is. It is about Miss Williams, I am sure. Miss Betsy Williams. She is a relation of the Colonel's, my dear; a very *near* relation. She is his natural daughter.

ELINOR. Indeed!

MRS JENNINGS. Oh, yes, 'twas a very tragic romance between him and her mother. Eliza was her name, I think.

SIR JOHN. Oh dear, this is unfortunate. How regretful. However, we are all together...why should we not drive about the countryside? We shall determine to be extremely merry all day long! *(To a SERVANT.)* Bring our carriages round!

(The "carriages" arrive.)

MARIANNE. Willoughby's was first!

WILLOUGHBY. and Marianne never looked happier than when she got into it.

MARIANNE. He drove through the park very fast,

ELINOR. and they were soon out of sight!

(WILLOUGHBY and MARIANNE exit in "the carriage.")

ELINOR. Alone...together.

MRS JENNINGS. Ah, Mr. Imprudence! I say one month before we see them wed!

(All exit but ELINOR.)

ELINOR. Elinor wondered at the strange and extraordinary silence of her sister and Willoughby on one particular subject. Why they should not openly acknowledge their engagement, at least to her mother and herself, Elinor could not imagine...and she began to doubt of their being really engaged.

Scene Sixteen

(Transition to Barton Cottage. **MRS DASHWOOD**, **MARGARET**, **WILLOUGHBY**, *and* **MARIANNE** *enter with books, sewing things, etc.)*

MRS DASHWOOD. Nothing could be more expressive of attachment to them all,

MARIANNE. than Willoughby's behaviour.

WILLOUGHBY. He seemed to consider and love the cottage as his home!

MRS DASHWOOD. You'll be happy to hear then that I intend to improve the cottage in the spring.

WILLOUGHBY. What! Improve this dear cottage! No. *That* I will never consent to. Not a stone should be moved.

MRS DASHWOOD. Willoughby, are you really so attached to this place as to see no defect in it?

WILLOUGHBY. I am. To me it is faultless. Nay, more, I consider it as the only form of building in which happiness is attainable, and were I rich enough I would instantly pull Combe Magna down, and build it up again in the exact plan of this cottage.

ELINOR. With dark narrow stairs and a kitchen that smokes, I suppose?

WILLOUGHBY. Yes, with all and every thing belonging to it. Then, I might perhaps be as happy at Combe Magna as I have been at Barton. This place will always have *one* claim of my affection, which no other can possibly share… And yet this house you would spoil, Mrs. Dashwood?

MRS DASHWOOD. Mrs. Dashwood assured him that no alteration should be attempted.

WILLOUGHBY. Tell me that not only your house will remain the same, but that I shall ever find you and yours *as* unchanged; and that you will always consider me with the kindness which has made everything belonging to you so dear to me.

MRS DASHWOOD. The promise was readily given!

Scene Seventeen

(Barton Cottage.)

MARIANNE. The next day, Marianne excused herself from the morning visit to Barton Park

> *(**MARIANNE** moves to **WILLOUGHBY**. The rest of the family takes a walk around the stage.)*

ELINOR. under a trifling *pretext* of employment.

MRS DASHWOOD. Willoughby must have promised to call on Marianne this morning! Oh girls, today may be the day!

(Calling out.) On their return!

> *(**MARIANNE**, sobbing, runs across the stage and exits. **WILLOUGHBY** slowly follows her.)*

MRS DASHWOOD. Willoughby, is anything the matter? Is Marianne ill?

WILLOUGHBY. I hope not. This is a heavy disappointment. My aunt has this morning exercised the privilege of riches upon a poor dependent cousin, by sending me on business to London.

MRS DASHWOOD. To London! And are you going this morning?

WILLOUGHBY. Almost this moment.

MRS DASHWOOD. This is very unfortunate. Your business will not detain you from us long I hope.

WILLOUGHBY. You are very kind, but I have no idea of returning into Devonshire immediately.

MRS DASHWOOD. Oh...well, you will always be welcome at Barton cottage, Willoughby.

WILLOUGHBY. My engagements at present are of such a nature—that—I dare not flatter myself...it is folly to linger in this manner! I will not torment myself any longer. Good day.

> *(**WILLOUGHBY** exits. **MARGARET** follows him.)*

MARGARET. Willoughby!

MRS DASHWOOD. What can it be? Can they have quarreled?

ELINOR. I can hardly account for it.

MRS DASHWOOD. Perhaps his aunt disapproves of their engagement?

ELINOR. if they ARE engaged

MRS DASHWOOD. My dear child, how can you—

ELINOR. I want no proof of their *affection*, but of their engagement I do.

MRS DASHWOOD. I am perfectly satisfied of both.

ELINOR. Yet not a syllable has been said to you on the subject, by either of them.

MRS DASHWOOD. I have not wanted syllables where actions have spoken so plainly. Has not his behavior to Marianne and to all of us, for at least the last fortnight, declared that he loved and considered her as his future wife? Elinor, is it possible to doubt their engagement? How could such a thought occur to you? Do you suppose him really indifferent to her?

ELINOR. No, he must and does love her, I am sure.

>   (**MARIANNE** *enters dramatically.*)

MRS DASHWOOD. Marianne?

MARIANNE. Marianne would have been ashamed to look her family in the face had she been able to sleep at all the first night after parting from Willoughby. (**MARIANNE** *bursts into tears.*)

MRS DASHWOOD. When breakfast was over

ELINOR. she walked out by herself,

MARIANNE. indulging the recollection of past enjoyment.

ELINOR. The evening passed off in an equal indulgence of feeling.

MARIANNE. and this *nourishment* of grief was every day applied.

ELINOR. No letter from Willoughby came;

>   (**MARIANNE** *exits.*)

and none seemed expected by Marianne. Mama, why do *you* not ask Marianne at once whether she is engaged to Willoughby? She used to be all unreserve, and to you more especially.

MRS DASHWOOD. I would not ask such a question for the world. Supposing it possible that they are *not* engaged, what distress would not such an enquiry inflict!

(**MRS DASHWOOD** *exits.*)

Scene Eighteen

(Barton Cottage. A week later. **MARGARET** *enters.)*

MARGARET. There is a gentleman approaching! Come look…

    *(***MARIANNE*** *enters.)*

MARIANNE. Willoughby! I knew how soon he would come!

    *(***MARGARET*** *runs back outside.* **ELINOR** *and* **MARIANNE** *look out the window.)*

ELINOR. The person is not tall enough for Willoughby, and has not his air.

MARGARET. *(From offstage.)* Edward! *C'est Edouard!*

    *(***ELINOR*** *and* **MARIANNE** *collect themselves.* **MARGARET** *and* **EDWARD** *enter.)*

MARIANNE. He was welcomed by them all with great cordiality!

ELINOR. but especially by Marianne,

MARIANNE. who showed more warmth of regard in her reception of him than even Elinor herself.

EDWARD. On Edward's side,

MARIANNE. there was a deficiency of all that a *lover* ought to look and say on such an occasion.

EDWARD. He was confused,

ELINOR. seemed scarcely sensible of pleasure in seeing them,

EDWARD. looked neither rapturous nor gay, and said little.

MARIANNE. Marianne began almost to feel a *dislike* of Edward. Did you come directly from London?

EDWARD. Ah, no, I have been in Devonshire a…uh a fortnight.

MARIANNE. A fortnight!

EDWARD. Yes, I have been staying with some friends near Plymouth.

ELINOR. …Oh, Plymouth.

EDWARD. Yes… Plymouth.

ELINOR. Edward was not entirely in spirits.

EDWARD. So…have you an agreeable neighborhood here? Are Sir John and Lady Middleton pleasant people?

MARIANNE. No, not at all, we could not be more unfortunately situated.

ELINOR. Marianne! How can you say so? They are a very respectable family, Mr. Ferrars; and towards us have behaved in the friendliest manner!

(**MRS DASHWOOD** *enters.*)

MRS DASHWOOD. Edward! Such a wonderful surprise! How delightful to see you! How are you dear?

EDWARD. His shyness could not stand against such a reception.

MRS DASHWOOD. How is your mother, Edward? Does Mrs. Ferrars still plan for you to be a great politician? Prime Minister perhaps?

EDWARD. No. I hope my mother is convinced that I have no inclination for a public life! Thank Heaven! I cannot be forced into genius and eloquence.

MRS DASHWOOD. You are too modest.

EDWARD. I wish as well as everybody else to be perfectly *happy*; but it must be in my own way. Greatness will not make me so.

MARIANNE. Strange that it would! What have wealth or grandeur to do with happiness?

MARGARET. I wish, that somebody would give us all a large fortune apiece!

MARIANNE. Oh that they would!

(**ELINOR** *and* **EDWARD** *laugh, sharing the joke.*)

EDWARD. What magnificent orders would travel from this family to London in such an event! What a happy day for print, book and music sellers! Or perhaps, Marianne, you would bestow your fortune as a reward on that person who wrote the ablest defense of your favorite maxim, that no one can ever be in love more than once in their life. Your opinion on that point is unchanged, I presume?

MARIANNE. Undoubtedly. At my time of life opinions are tolerably fixed. It is not likely that I should now see or hear any thing to change them.

ELINOR. Marianne is as steadfast as ever, you see.

MARIANNE. Oh, I forgot. It is Elinor's preference that I'd be guided wholly by the opinions of other people – of our neighbors.

ELINOR. No Marianne, never. Though I confess to having often wished you to treat our general acquaintance with greater attention.

EDWARD. You have not been able to bring your sister over to your plan of general civility?

ELINOR. Quite the contrary.

EDWARD. I never wish to offend, but I am so foolishly shy, that I fear I seem negligent to my acquaintances.

MARIANNE. No, Edward, you are simply reserved.

EDWARD. Reserved! Am I reserved, Marianne?

MARIANNE. Yes, very.

EDWARD. Reserved? How, in what manner? What am I to tell you? What can you suppose?

ELINOR. ...Oh, Marianne calls every one reserved who does not talk as fast, and admire what she admires as rapturously as herself.

MARIANNE. *(Notices a ring* **EDWARD** *is now wearing.)* I never saw you wear a ring before, Edward. Is that Fanny's hair? I should have thought her hair had been darker.

EDWARD. Yes...it is my sister's hair. The setting casts a different shade on it, you know.

ELINOR. Elinor met his eye. That the hair was her own, she instantaneously knew

MARIANNE. As did Marianne!

ELINOR. The only difference

MARIANNE. was that, Marianne considered it as a free gift from her sister

ELINOR. but Elinor knew it had been procured by some theft or contrivance unknown to herself. She did not, however, regard it as an affront.

EDWARD. Edward remained only a few days at Barton.

MRS DASHWOOD. Please stay, Edward! We are so happy to have your company.

EDWARD. Thank you, Mrs. Dashwood. Truly my greatest happiness is in being here with you, but I must go.

ELINOR. Edward seemed resolved to be gone when his enjoyment among his friends was at the height.

EDWARD. These days have passed so quickly. I grow more partial to this cottage and its environs *(Sigh.)* I don't know where I'm... I'm wholly without purpose.

MARGARET. Then don't go, Edward.

EDWARD. Oh, Miss Margaret I must... I must. To Norland or London I'll go I suppose.

*(Bow/curtsy. **EDWARD** exits.)*

MARIANNE. Why did Edward come if not to...?

ELINOR. Elinor sat down to her drawing as soon as Edward was out of the house, busily employing herself the whole day

MARIANNE. and neither sought nor avoided the mention of his name. Such *calm* behavior as this! Shocking!

*(**THOMAS** enters with a letter, delivers it and exits.)*

From London, Thomas?! It is Willoughby! Oh...no.

*(**MARIANNE** hands the letter to **ELINOR**.)*

ELINOR. Sir John and Lady Middleton have invited us to a dinner party. Mrs. Jennings' other daughter and son-in-law, Mr. and Mrs. Palmer, are visiting...and also a cousin from Exeter.

MARIANNE. Why should they ask us? The rent of this cottage is said to be low; but we have it on very hard terms, if we are to dine at the park whenever we are asked.

Scene Nineteen

(Transition to Barton Park. **MRS JENNINGS**, **SIR JOHN**, **MR PALMER**, **MRS PALMER**, *who is heavily pregnant,* **LUCY**, **MARGARET**, **MRS DASHWOOD**, *and* **SERVANTS** *enter.)*

SIR JOHN. I told you they are lovely did I not?

MRS JENNINGS. Good evening, my dears! You must meet my younger daughter and her husband.

SIR JOHN. A surprise visit!

MRS JENNINGS. I thought I heard a carriage last night, while we were drinking our tea, but it never entered my head that it could be them! My daughter, Mrs. Palmer

MRS PALMER. *(Curtsy.)* greeted them with a smile

ELINOR. and smiled all evening long,

MRS PALMER. except when she laughed. *(*MRS PALMER *laughs.)*

MRS JENNINGS. *(Introducing* MR PALMER.*)* Mr. Palmer

MR PALMER. *(Bows, then sits and reads the paper.)* was a grave looking man with an air of self-consequence and sense but of little willingness to please or be pleased.

SIR JOHN. *(Introducing* LUCY.*)* And we brought you a new companion from Exeter—Miss Lucy Steele! A cousin of Mrs. Jennings.

(Bows/curtsies all around.)

LUCY. Miss Lucy Steele had a sharp quick eye and a smartness of air, which

MARIANNE. though it did not give actual elegance or grace,

ELINOR. gave distinction to her person.

*(*MRS PALMER *sits between* LUCY, ELINOR, *and* MARGARET. MARIANNE *gazes out the window.* MRS DASHWOOD *chats with* MRS JENNINGS.*)*

MRS PALMER. I am so glad to see you! For it is so bad a day I was afraid you might not come, which would be a shocking thing, as we've heard so much about you.

I just knew I had to know you as soon as possible. And we are going into town this winter, you know, so we shall meet again there I hope.

ELINOR. Oh no, we are not going to London.

MRS PALMER. Not go to London! I shall be quite disappointed if you do not. Should not you, Mr. Palmer? Mr. Palmer does not hear me. He never does sometimes. Is there any news in the paper, my dear?

MR PALMER. *(continuing to read)* No, none at all. Do you think this rain will continue for another fortnight, Sir John? Such weather makes every thing and everybody disgusting.

SIR JOHN. I am afraid, Miss Marianne, with this rain, you have not been able to take your usual walk to Allenham today.

         (MARIANNE is silent.)

MRS PALMER. Oh, don't be so sly before us, for we know all about Willoughby, I assure you; and I admire your taste very much, for I think he is extremely handsome. We do not live a great way from him in the country, Combe Magna, you know. Not above ten miles, I dare say.

         (MARIANNE takes notice.)

MR PALMER. Much nearer thirty.

MRS PALMER. Ah, well! there is not much difference. I never was at his house; but they say it is a sweet pretty place.

MR PALMER. As vile a spot as I ever saw in my life.

MRS PALMER. Is it very ugly? Then it must be some other place that is so pretty I suppose.

MR PALMER. You *would* suppose so.

MRS PALMER. *(Laughing.)* Mr. Palmer is so droll! He is always out of humor.

        *(**MRS PALMER** laughs and crosses to **MR PALMER** and **MRS JENNINGS**.)*

ELINOR. It was impossible for anyone to be more thoroughly good-natured, or more determined to be happy than Mrs. Palmer.

LUCY. Such a shame Lady Middleton is indisposed.

> *(We hear one of the children yelling or crying offstage.)*

Oh but her children! An't they delightful, Miss Dashwood? I never saw such fine children in my life. I declare I quite dote upon them already! An't they such angels!

> *(**MARIANNE** smiles and looks to **ELINOR**.)*

ELINOR. The whole task of telling lies when politeness required it always fell upon Elinor.

LUCY. And Sir John too, what a *charming* man he is!

> *(**MARIANNE** curtsies and crosses to play the pianoforte.)*

LUCY. And how do you like Devonshire, Miss Dashwood? I suppose you was very sorry to leave Sussex.

ELINOR. *(Surprised.)* I...yes I was.

LUCY. I have heard Sir John admire Norland excessively.

ELINOR. Oh! Of course, I think every one *must* admire it, who ever saw the place.

LUCY. The remoteness of Barton must come as a surprise to you as it did me. I am accustomed to Exeter, you know. But we shall keep each other company shall we not?

MARGARET. *Ah mais oui! Certainment! Vous jouez le piano Mademoiselle Steele?*

ELINOR. *(Beat.)* Do you play, Miss Steele?

LUCY. I...never learned music.

MARGARET. You certainly paint then?

LUCY. Well...

MARGARET. Elinor and I are now reading *As You Like it*. Rosalind is the greatest female character in Shakespeare's canon, do not you think?

LUCY. His...cannon?

ELINOR. Was your journey to Barton Park uneventful, Miss Steele?

LUCY. Delightfully so! Though it is not considered an easy journey. And I do not wish to leave soon as I expect to be very much occupied with Lady Middleton and her children. Such delights!

ELINOR. Indeed.

> *(Applause after* **MARIANNE***'s performance.* **MRS JENNINGS** *and* **SIR JOHN** *approach.)*

LUCY. The visit of Miss Lucy Steele at Barton Park

MRS JENNINGS. was lengthened far beyond what the first invitation implied.

SIR JOHN. Her favor increased!

MRS JENNINGS. She could not be spared!

SIR JOHN. In the end, Miss Steele was prevailed on to stay

LUCY. nearly two *months* at Barton Park!

Scene Twenty

(Transition. Different party. Same place. Same people. Everyone mingles. **LUCY** *corners* **ELINOR**.*)*

ELINOR. Miss Steele never missed an opportunity of engaging Elinor in conversation.

LUCY. Her want of information, in the most common particulars,

ELINOR. could not be concealed from Elinor

LUCY. in spite of her constant endeavor to appear to advantage. Pray, Miss Dashwood, are you personally acquainted with your sister-in-law's mother, Mrs. Ferrars?

ELINOR. With my...with Fanny's mother? No, I have never seen Mrs. Ferrars.

LUCY. No indeed? I wonder at that. Then you cannot tell me what sort of a woman she is?

ELINOR. No, I know nothing of her.

LUCY. I am sure you think me very strange for enquiring and I cannot bear to be thought impertinent by you whose good opinion is so well worth having. You see— Mrs. Ferrars is certainly nothing to me at present—but the time MAY come—when we may be very...*intimately* connected.

ELINOR. Miss Steele looked down

LUCY. with one side glance at her companion to observe its effect on her.

ELINOR. Good heavens! Are you acquainted with Mr. Robert Ferrars?

LUCY. No, I never saw Robert Ferrars in my life; but with his elder brother, Edward.

ELINOR. What felt Elinor at that moment.

LUCY. You may well be surprised as it is a great secret. Not a soul knows of it. Edward and I have been *engaged* these four years. He were under my uncle's tutelage, you know, a considerable while—my uncle...who lives near *Plymouth*. I was very unwilling to enter into an engagement without the approval of his mother; but I was too young, and loved him too well, to be prudent. Though you do not know him so well as me, Miss Dashwood, you must be sensible that he is very capable of making a woman sincerely attached to him.

ELINOR. Certainly... I confess myself so surprised by what you tell me. Engaged to Mr. Edward Ferrars. I beg your pardon; but surely there must be some mistake of person or name. We cannot mean the same Mr. Ferrars.

LUCY. We can mean no other. The brother of your sister-in-law, Mrs. John Dashwood. To prevent the possibility of a mistake, be so good as to look at his face.

> (**LUCY** *produces a painted miniature from her purse and shows it to* **ELINOR**.)

ELINOR. Elinor's security sunk; but her self-command did not sink with it. Four years you have been engaged?

LUCY. Yes; and heaven knows how much longer we may have to wait. I have no fortune and his mother would certainly not approve. Poor Edward! It puts him quite out of heart. I gave him a lock of my hair set in a ring when I saw him last, and that were some comfort to him. Perhaps you might have noticed the ring when you saw him?

ELINOR. ...I did.

> (*Light special/private moment.*)

Elinor felt a distress and mortification beyond anything she had ever felt before. Had Edward been intentionally deceiving her? Was this an engagement of the heart? No, whatever it might once have been—his affection was all her own. Elinor could not be deceived in that. Edward certainly loved her. His melancholy state of mind and his uncertain behavior towards herself... all became clear. He had been blamable but if he had injured *her*, how much more had he injured *himself*? A wife like Lucy Steele?

Elinor wept for him.

(Light special out.)

LUCY. As I said, Edward is entirely dependent on his mother. He has nothing of his own so...we have resolved to wait. But Edward's love for me has stood the trial of our separation so well. I can safely say he has never gave me one moment's alarm. I am rather of a jealous temper by nature, you see. Oh, I'm desperate to get to London this winter as Edward will be there with your brother- and sister-in-law.

ELINOR. I see.

*(**MRS JENNINGS** and **MRS PALMER** approach.)*

LUCY. I have no doubt in the world of your faithfully keeping this secret!

ELINOR. ...Of course.

MRS PALMER. Thick as thieves you two are!

MRS JENNINGS. Yes, such dear friends! You know... I'm traveling to town this week and I've a good mind to take you *all* off to London with me.

MARIANNE. *(Taking notice.)* London?!

MRS JENNINGS. The Miss Dashwoods *and* Miss Steele— you'll be the talk of the town.

MRS PALMER. Yes indeed, and *I* am determined to meet you there this winter!

LUCY. Oh yes, London!

*(**MARIANNE** approaches.)*

ELINOR. Thank you so very much, Mrs. Jennings, but we cannot leave our mother at this time.

MRS JENNINGS. Oh, Lord! Your mother can spare you very well!

MRS PALMER. Yes indeed! Miss Steele, you shall stay with us and the Dashwoods with Mama. You must come to London Miss Dashwood! Mr. Palmer, my love...don't *you* long to have the Miss Dashwoods meet us in town?

MR PALMER. *(entirely disinterested)* Certainly, I came into Devonshire with no other view.

MRS PALMER. There now! You see, Mr. Palmer expects you; so you cannot refuse to come!

(**MRS DASHWOOD** *and* **MARGARET** *approach.*)

MRS JENNINGS. I have had such good luck getting my own children off my hands that if I don't get one of you at least well married before the season is over, it shall not be my fault!

MARIANNE. I thank you, ma'am, sincerely thank you. Your invitation has ensured my gratitude forever, and it would give me such happiness!

ELINOR. But Marianne, Mama is—

MARIANNE. Oh we shall miss Mama and Margaret terribly, but you do not object do you Mama? How could you when we will be taken care of and overseen by Mrs. Jennings?

MRS DASHWOOD. Mrs. Dashwood did not object. Elinor, do not fret over your mother. Margaret and I will be very content together at Barton.

MRS JENNINGS. Delightful! We are set upon it then!

MARIANNE. Marianne's joy was almost a degree beyond happiness!

ELINOR. This eagerness declared Marianne's dependence on finding Willoughby in London.

(*All exit excitedly, leaving* **ELINOR** *alone onstage.*)

MARIANNE. (*To* **MRS DASHWOOD** *as they exit.*) But oh Mama, how painful shall be our separation—we will write you every day!

ELINOR. And within a week... Elinor found herself on the road to London.

(*blackout*)

End of Act I

ACT II

Scene One

*(**MRS JENNINGS**' house in London. Lights up on **MRS JENNINGS** showing **ELINOR** and **MARIANNE** into their room. **SERVANT** attends them. **MARIANNE** goes to the desk, finds paper, and immediately begins writing a letter.)*

MRS JENNINGS. Mrs. Jennings' house in London was very handsome!

ELINOR. Elinor and Marianne were put in possession of a very comfortable apartment.

*(**MRS JENNINGS** exits.)*

I was just going to write home, Marianne. Had not you better defer your letter for a day or two?

MARIANNE. I am not writing to my mother.

*(**MARIANNE** folds letter then hands it to **SERVANT** who exits.)*

ELINOR. To Willoughby then...they ARE engaged!

MARIANNE. Marianne could hardly eat any dinner and instead spent much of her time pacing the drawing room until

ELINOR. They heard a decided rap at the door.

MARIANNE. Oh, Elinor, it is Willoughby, indeed it is!

ELINOR. Marianne seemed almost ready to throw herself into his arms when—

*(**SERVANT** shows in **BRANDON**.)*

SERVANT. Colonel Brandon

MARIANNE. It was too great a shock to be born with calmness!

>   (**MARIANNE** *exits quickly.*)

BRANDON. Is your sister ill?

ELINOR. She is, indeed…a headache. The journey from Barton has left her quite fatigued. What a pleasure to see you, Colonel Brandon.

>   (*Bow/curtsy.*)

BRANDON. Yes, Miss Dashwood, a pleasure indeed. How was your journey?

ELINOR. In this calm, dispirited, kind of way they continued to talk. Have you been in London ever since we saw you last?

BRANDON. Yes, almost ever since. *(Beat.)* Forgive me, when am I to congratulate you?

ELINOR. I'm sorry?

BRANDON. Your sister's engagement to Mr. Willoughby is very generally known.

ELINOR. It cannot be generally known for her own family do not know it.

BRANDON. I beg your pardon, but they openly correspond and their marriage is universally talked of.

ELINOR. How can that be? By whom can you have heard it mentioned?

BRANDON. By many, some with whom you are most intimate. Is everything finally settled? Is it impossible to—? I have no right—excuse me, Miss Dashwood, I hardly know what to do, and on your prudence I have the strongest dependence. Tell me that it is all absolutely resolved on—that concealment of my feelings, if possible, is all that remains.

ELINOR. I have never been informed of an engagement… however I am convinced of their mutual affection.

BRANDON. I see. To your sister I wish all imaginable happiness; to Willoughby that he may endeavor to *deserve* her!

(Bow/curtsy. **BRANDON** *exits.)*

ELINOR. Elinor derived no comfortable feelings from *this* conversation.

Scene Two

(The next day. **MRS JENNINGS** *and* **MARIANNE**
enter.)

MRS JENNINGS. The next morning!

MARIANNE. Marianne awoke with recovered spirits and
happy looks.

ELINOR. The disappointment of the evening before
seemed forgotten in the expectation of what was to
happen that day.

MARIANNE. Has the post yet arrived?

MRS JENNINGS. Yes, dear.

MARIANNE. Was there…anything for me?

MRS JENNINGS. I'm sorry, Miss Marianne, not yet.

*(***MRS PALMER*** and* **LUCY** *enter.)*

MRS PALMER. Helloooooooooooooo. Mama! Miss Dashwood!
Miss Marianne!

MRS JENNINGS. Oh, good morning my dears! To Bond
Street, ladies!

*(Transition. Bond Street. The ladies stroll, perhaps
with parasols.)*

MARIANNE. Wherever they went, Marianne was on the
watch.

ELINOR. If Marianne had not known Willoughby to be in
town she would not have written to him as she did. And
if he IS in town, how odd that he should neither come
nor write!

MRS PALMER. Miss Steele, look at that hat!

MRS JENNINGS. Oh, If this delightful weather holds much
longer, Sir John will not like leaving Barton next week;
'tis a sad thing for sportsmen to lose a day's pleasure.

MARIANNE. That is true. I had not thought of that. This
good weather will keep many sportsmen in the country.

MRS JENNINGS. It cannot be expected to last long, however.

MARIANNE. No, no, at this time of year…frosts will soon set in. In another day or two perhaps—nay, perhaps it may freeze tonight!

LUCY. *(Sidling up to* **ELINOR.***)* Miss Dashwood! You are enjoying your time in London, I daresay.

ELINOR. Yes, Miss Steele, thank you. And you?

LUCY. Oh yes! Edward will soon be arriving with his sister and your brother. I'm so anxious to see him and yet it is too terrifying. What if we are found out?!

ELINOR. Indeed…that is much to consider.

MRS JENNINGS. It was late in the morning before they returned to Mrs. Jennings'

> *(Transition back to* **MRS JENNINGS**' *house.* **SERVANT** *enters to take their coats or bonnets, etc.)*

ELINOR. and no sooner had they entered the house

MARIANNE. Has no letter been left here for me since we went out?

SERVANT. No, Miss.

MARIANNE. Are you quite sure of it? Are you certain that no servant, no porter has left any letter or note?

SERVANT. None have, Miss.

MARIANNE. How very odd!

ELINOR. How odd, indeed.

MRS PALMER. Mama, when is tea?

MRS JENNINGS. Now darling. Mark my words…it is the good weather, Miss Marianne! Our sportsmen shall arrive in town soon!

MARIANNE. Yes.

> *(***ALL** *exit with* **JENNINGS** *except* **ELINOR** *and* **MARIANNE.***)*

ELINOR. Elinor immediately wrote to her mother and urgently begged her to demand from Marianne, an account of her real situation with respect to Willoughby.

MARIANNE. It was about a week after their arrival,

ELINOR. following a morning's walk

MARIANNE. Don't you find it colder than it was yesterday, Elinor?

(**SERVANT** *enters with a card and a letter.*)

SERVANT. This card was on the table, Miss.

MARIANNE. It is from Willoughby! Good God. He has been here while we were out!

ELINOR. Oh dearest! Depend upon it, he will call again tomorrow.

MARIANNE. Is this for me?

SERVANT. No, ma'am, for my mistress.

MARIANNE. *(Takes the note anyway.)* It is indeed for Mrs. Jennings; how provoking!

(**MARIANNE** *returns note to* **SERVANT** *who exits.*)

ELINOR. You are expecting a letter then?

MARIANNE. Yes, a little – not much.

ELINOR. You have no confidence in me, Marianne.

MARIANNE. Nay, Elinor, this reproach from you—you who have confidence in no one!

ELINOR. Me…indeed, Marianne, I have nothing to tell.

MARIANNE. Nor I. We have neither of us any thing to tell; you, because you do not communicate, and I, because I conceal nothing.

(**MARIANNE** *paces, perhaps looking out a window from time to time.*)

ELINOR. Too restless for employment

MARIANNE. Too anxious for conversation, Marianne's mind was never quiet. She could not read. She could not play. The expectation of seeing Willoughby every hour of the day made her unfit for anything.

ELINOR. Three or four days passed with no word…

Scene Three

(Transition to London ball. **MRS JENNINGS** *enters.)*

MRS JENNINGS. They were engaged to a party!

*(***LUCY, BRANDON*** *and* ***SIR JOHN*** *enter. All other available cast members are party guests or* ***SERVANTS***.*)*

SIR JOHN. Mrs. Jennings!

MRS JENNINGS. Sir John! I see the cold weather has finally brought you to town!

SIR JOHN. You all look so lovely! Lovely lovely lovely!

BRANDON. Miss Dashwood. Miss Marianne.

(Bows/curtsies.)

LUCY. Miss Dashwood. Are you *still* enjoying London?

ELINOR. Yes, Miss Steele, very much.

LUCY. I've left the Palmers and I'm staying with Sir John and Lady Middleton now, you know.

ELINOR. Indeed? That must be very enjoyable.

LUCY. I suppose you will go and stay with your brother and sister, Miss Dashwood, when they come to town.

ELINOR. No… I do not think we shall.

LUCY. Oh, yes, I dare say you will.

*(***JOHN*** *and* ***FANNY DASHWOOD*** *and* ***ROBERT FERRARS*** *stumble upon them.)*

JOHN. Elinor! Well, hello.

ELINOR. John. Fanny. *(Curtsy.)* May I introduce you to Miss Steele.

FANNY. Delighted.

(Bows/curtsies.)

JOHN. Miss Steele. My brother-in-law, Mr. Robert Ferrars. Miss Dashwood and Miss Steele.

ROBERT. A pleasure ladies.

(**ROBERT** *bows in an extremely pretentious, almost ridiculous manner.*)

JOHN. …We wished very much to call upon you yesterday but it was impossible as we spent the day with Mrs. Ferrars. THIS morning I had fully intended to call on you but one has always so much to do on first coming to town. Tomorrow I think I shall certainly be able to call on you and be introduced to your friend, Mrs. Jennings. I understand she is a woman of very good fortune.

FANNY. And the Middletons too, you must introduce us to them.

JOHN. Yes, they are excellent neighbors to you in the country, we understand.

ELINOR. Excellent indeed, in fact—

JOHN. I am extremely glad to hear it. But so it ought to be; they are people of large fortune, they are related to you, and every accommodation that can serve to make your situation pleasant might be reasonably expected. You are most comfortably settled in your little cottage?

(**MARIANNE** *approaches during the following.*)

ROBERT. I am excessively fond of a cottage; there is always so much comfort, so much space, so much elegance about them. And I protest, if I had any money to spare, I should buy a little land and build one myself. I advise everybody who is going to build, to build a cottage.

JOHN. Edward brought us a most charming account of the place.

MARIANNE. Edward? Is he in town?

FANNY. *(Coldly.)* Good evening Miss Marianne… Yes, Edward is newly arrived. He is staying with our mother, Mrs. Ferrars.

MARIANNE. Delightful! I long to see Edward.

JOHN. His brother, Mr. Robert Ferrars. Miss Marianne Dashwood.

(Bow/curtsy.)

FANNY. So, Miss Steele, how are you acquainted with…the Miss Dashwoods?

> *(**FANNY** and **LUCY** move up stage to silently chat. **MARIANNE** moves up stage to silently introduce **JOHN** to **SIR JOHN**, **BRANDON** and **MRS JENNINGS**. **ELINOR** and **ROBERT** find themselves together.)*

ROBERT. It must be quite a surprise to you, Miss Dashwood, that Edward Ferrars and I are brothers.

ELINOR. Yes. It is to be wondered at.

ROBERT. I know him to be a very good-hearted creature and well meaning but, alas, the GAUCHERIE! He is not here this evening as such gatherings make him quite uncomfortable. Yet…

> *(**ROBERT** gestures to himself as if to say "Not me!")*

I am certain our differences are due entirely to the misfortune of a private education and not to any natural deficiency. I, myself benefited merely from the advantage of a public school, and am as well fitted to mix in the world as any other man!

ELINOR. Elinor merely smiled for she did not think he deserved the compliment of rational opposition.

> *(**FANNY** gets **ROBERT**'s attention and they silently converse with **LUCY**. **MARIANNE** crosses to **ELINOR**. **WILLOUGHBY** is revealed nearby with a group which includes **MISS GREY**.)*

MARIANNE. Suddenly,

ELINOR. They perceived… Willoughby, standing within a few yards of them,

MARIANNE. *(To **ELINOR**.)* Good heavens! he is there—he is there! Oh! why does he not look at me?

ELINOR. Pray, pray be composed, and do not betray what you feel to everybody present. Perhaps he has not observed you yet.

MARIANNE. *(Unable to wait any longer.)* Willoughby?!

(MARIANNE holds out her hand to WILLOUGHBY who approaches, does not take her hand and speaks to ELINOR. He bows slightly.)

WILLOUGHBY. Miss Dashwood, hello…May I enquire after your mother?

ELINOR. She is well, sir.

WILLOUGHBY. How long have you been in town?

MARIANNE. *(Beat.)* Good God! Willoughby, what is the meaning of this? Have you not received my letters? Will you not shake hands with me?

(WILLOUGHBY takes MARIANNE's hand for a second.)

ELINOR. Her touch seemed painful to him,

WILLOUGHBY. I did myself the honor of calling on you last Tuesday, and very much regretted that I was not fortunate enough to find yourselves and Mrs. Jennings at home. My card was not lost, I hope.

MARIANNE. But have you not received my notes? Here is some mistake I am sure—some dreadful mistake. Tell me, Willoughby; for heaven's sake tell me, what is the matter?

(People are starting to notice.)

WILLOUGHBY. Yes, I had the pleasure of receiving the information of your arrival in town, which you were so good as to send me.

(WILLOUGHBY quickly bows and returns to his group.)

MARIANNE. Go to him, Elinor, and force him to come to me. Tell him I must see him again—must speak to him instantly. I shall not have a moment's peace till this is explained—some dreadful misapprehension or other. Oh go to him this moment.

ELINOR. No, my dearest Marianne, you must wait. This is not a place for explanations. Wait…

(MARIANNE gently faints in ELINOR's arms. Friends rush to them as blackout.)

Scene Four

> (**MRS JENNINGS** ' *house. Lights up on* **ELINOR** *and* **MARIANNE** *who is writing.*)

ELINOR. Marianne, may I ask—?

MARIANNE. No, Elinor, ask nothing; you will soon know all.

ELINOR. Darling…

MARIANNE. Please, do not speak to me for the world!

> (**MARIANNE** *exits with the letter.* **MRS JENNINGS** *enters.*)

MRS JENNINGS. Breakfast was Mrs. Jennings favorite meal!

ELINOR. And it lasted a considerable time.

> (*A door bell is heard.* **SERVANT** *enters with a thick letter.* **MARIANNE** *enters, grabs letter and exits.*)

MRS JENNINGS. From Willoughby no doubt. Upon my word, I never saw a young woman so desperately in love in my life! Miss Marianne is quite an altered creature. I hope, from the bottom of my heart, he won't keep her waiting much longer, for it is quite grievous to see her look so ill and forlorn. Pray, when are they to be married?

ELINOR. Please excuse me.

> (*Transition to Bedroom.* **ELINOR** *crosses to the bedroom.* **MRS JENNINGS** *exits.* **MARIANNE**, *sobbing, has several letters and the lock of hair.*)

Elinor, knew that such grief, shocking as it was to witness it, must have its course.

> (**MARIANNE** *reads one of the letters.*)

MARIANNE. MY DEAR MADAM, I have just had the honor of receiving your letter. I am much concerned to find there was anything in my behavior last night that did not meet your approval.

> (**WILLOUGHBY** *appears in light special.* **MARIANNE** *gives letter to* **ELINOR**.)

WILLOUGHBY. Though I am quite at a loss to discover in what point I could be so unfortunate as to offend you, I entreat your forgiveness of what I can assure you was perfectly unintentional. I shall never reflect on my former acquaintance with your family without the most grateful pleasure. If I have been so unfortunate as to give rise to a belief of more than I felt, or meant to express, I shall reproach myself. That I should ever have meant more you will allow to be impossible, when you understand that my affections have been long engaged elsewhere.

(Light special out on **WILLOUGHBY**.*)*

ELINOR. I obey your commands in returning your letters and the lock of hair, which you so obligingly bestowed on me. Your most obedient humble Servant, John Willoughby. I never supposed him so cruel.

MARIANNE. Oh! Elinor!

*(***ELINOR*** *holds* **MARIANNE**.*)*

ELINOR. Darling, think if your engagement had been carried on for months and months.

MARIANNE. Engagement? There has been no engagement. He has broken no faith with me.

ELINOR. He told you that he loved you!

MARIANNE. Yes—no—never absolutely. It was every day implied, but never declared. Sometimes I thought it had been—but it never was.

ELINOR. But you *wrote* to him. I thought…

MARIANNE. He did love me Elinor! I know he did. *(***MARIANNE*** *sobs.)* Oh, Happy Elinor, YOU cannot have an idea of what I suffer. Edward loves you—what, oh what, can do away such happiness as that? You can have no grief. *(Sobs overtake her for a moment.)* Forgive me, forgive me. Elinor, I must go home. I must go to Mama. Cannot we be gone tomorrow?

ELINOR. Tomorrow, Marianne?

(MARIANNE dissolves into tears again. MRS JENNINGS tiptoes in.)

MRS JENNINGS. How is she, Miss Dashwood? Poor thing! she looks very bad. No wonder. I just heard Willoughby is to be married very soon to a Miss Grey—worth *fifty thousand* pounds! Ay, it is but too true. What a good-for-nothing fellow! Oh poor thing! I won't disturb her any longer, for she had better have her cry out at once and have done with.

(MRS JENNINGS exits.)

MARIANNE. Oh, I want to go home! I want Mama, Elinor! Please!

(MARIANNE runs off.)

Scene Five

(Transition to **MRS JENNINGS***' Drawing Room.*
BRANDON *appears.)*

BRANDON. How is Miss Marianne?

ELINOR. Not well. I must write my mother.

BRANDON. Willoughby...

ELINOR. You've heard. Of course. Till now, Marianne never doubted Willoughby's regard; but I am almost convinced that he never was really attached to her. There seems a hardness of heart about him.

BRANDON. And your sister—how did she—

ELINOR. She suffers severely but you know her disposition and may believe how eagerly she would still justify him if she could.

BRANDON. Miss Dashwood, my regard for Miss Marianne, for your family—will you allow me to prove it, by relating some circumstances which but an earnest desire of being useful—

ELINOR. You have something to tell me of Mr. Willoughby. Pray let me hear it.

BRANDON. You have probably entirely forgotten a conversation between us in which I alluded to a lady I had once known, as resembling, in some measure, your sister Marianne?

ELINOR. Indeed. I have not forgotten it.

BRANDON. Her name was Eliza. There is a very strong resemblance between your sister and Eliza—the same warmth of heart, the same eagerness of spirits. Growing up, I cannot remember the time when I did not love Eliza and she felt as passionately for me. Her story, though different than your sister's, was... no less unfortunate. At seventeen she was lost to me forever. We were within a few hours of eloping together when we were found out. I was banished to a distant relation and Eliza was married—married against her inclination to my older brother. Her fortune was large, and our family estate much encumbered. He did not deserve her; he did not even love her. He treated her… unkindly. I was sent off into the army only to return years later to learn of their *divorce* and her decline. After six months of fruitless search, I found Eliza wasting away in a debtor's prison. I shall not pain you with the tragic details for I *was* out of the country and… *(Beat.)*

Upon Eliza's *death* she left to my care her only child, a three-year-old girl—the offspring of her first seducer. Her name is Betsy, Betsy Williams. Her father, whoever he was, had disappeared. This girl, my little Betsy, was a precious trust to me. I adore her as if she were my own. She is now sixteen and lives under the care of a very respectable woman, but almost a twelvemonth back, while on holiday in Bath, Betsy *disappeared*. How I searched. What I feared and what I suffered.

ELINOR. Good heavens!

BRANDON. The first news that reached me of her arrived on the very morning of our intended party to Delaford; and was the reason of my leaving Barton so suddenly. Betsy was discovered…with child—in a situation so dire, with no creditable home, no help, no friends, ignorant of the father's whereabouts.

ELINOR. No, it could not be—not Willoughby.

BRANDON. You may guess what I have felt on seeing your sister as fond of Willoughby as ever, and on being assured that she was to marry him.

ELINOR. This is beyond anything.

BRANDON. Had I not seriously, and from my heart believed this information might be of service, might lessen Miss Marianne's regrets…

    *(**MARIANNE** enters unseen and watches this.)*

ELINOR. Of course. Thank you, Colonel Brandon. Thank you. Have you…seen Mr. Willoughby since you left us at Barton?

BRANDON. Yes. One meeting was unavoidable.

ELINOR. What! Have you met him to—

BRANDON. I could meet him in no other way. We met by appointment. We returned...unwounded, and the meeting, therefore, never got abroad.

ELINOR. Oh dear.

BRANDON. And now, Miss Dashwood, I shall leave you. I am dividing you from your sister and her care. Forgive me.

> (**BRANDON** *turns to go, sees* **MARIANNE**, *bows and exits.* **MARIANNE** *joins* **ELINOR**.)

ELINOR. Should I have told you dearest?

MARIANNE. Yes. That poor girl. Yes...thank you Elinor.

> (**MARIANNE** *and* **ELINOR** *exit. Three separate light specials on* **JENNINGS**, **SIR JOHN**, *and* **MRS PALMER**. *The following is delivered out to the audience.*)

MRS JENNINGS. The wedding ceremony occurred this very day. It's certain. Willoughby is a married man.

SIR JOHN. Poor Miss Marianne! And Willoughby, a man of whom I've always had such reason to think well! Such a remarkable hunter! I wish him at the devil with all my heart.

MRS PALMER. I hate him so much that I am resolved never to mention his name again, and I shall tell everybody I see, how good-for-nothing he is! I am determined to drop his acquaintance immediately, and I am very thankful that I have never been acquainted with him at all!

Scene Six

*(Light specials out. All exit. **MRS JENNINGS'**
house. **ELINOR** and **SERVANT** and **LUCY** enter
from opposite sides of the stage.)*

ELINOR. Early the next morning –

SERVANT. Miss Steele

*(**SERVANT** exits.)*

LUCY. My dear friend!

ELINOR. Hello Miss Steele.

LUCY. Your sister-in-law—Mrs. Fanny Dashwood…so
exceedingly affable! I dreaded meeting her but…
such kindness! No pride, no hauteur, all sweetness and
affability! And Edward's brother, Robert Ferrars…such
a gentleman! I wonder I should never hear you say how
agreeable Fanny Dashwood was?

She said more than once, she should always be glad to
see me, which will certainly put me in Edward's way.
I've not yet seen him but *now*—Oh such contentment!
Dear Elinor, I know you must be happy for me. Heaven
knows what I should have done without your friendship.
Next to Edward's love, it is the greatest comfort I have.

ELINOR. Elinor blushed for the insincerity of Edward's
future wife.

*(**SERVANT** enters followed by **EDWARD**. **SERVANT**
exits.)*

SERVANT. Mr. Ferrars.

EDWARD. Miss Dashwood—

*(**EDWARD** sees **LUCY**. Beat.)*

ELINOR. It was a very awkward moment.

LUCY. They were not only all three together,

EDWARD. but were together without the relief of any other
person.

ELINOR. Mr. Ferrars! I believe you know Miss Steele.

EDWARD. Uh yes… Miss Steele, how do you do?

>   *(Bow/curtsy.)*

ELINOR. My brother informed us you were newly in town. I am pleased to see you.

EDWARD. And I you—

LUCY. Lucy seemed determined to make no contribution to the comfort of the others, and would not say a word.

ELINOR. Mrs. Ferrars is well?

EDWARD. Yes-yes.

ELINOR. I'm glad to hear it. I know our mother would wish me to send her very best love to you.

EDWARD. Mrs. Dashwood is all kindness.

ELINOR. Oh, I'm not thinking. I must fetch Marianne. She will be delighted to see you. Excuse me.

>   *(**ELINOR** exits, **LUCY** steps toward **EDWARD**, **MARIANNE** rushes into the room followed by **ELINOR**.)*

MARIANNE. *(Taking his hand.)* Dear Edward! This is a moment of great happiness! This would almost make amends for everything.

EDWARD. Marianne, you… Is London agreeing with you Marianne?

MARIANNE. Oh, don't think of me! Don't think of *my* health. Elinor is well, you see. That must be enough for us both.

EDWARD. Do you *like* London?

MARIANNE. Not at all. The sight of you, Edward, is the only comfort it has afforded; and thank Heaven you are what you always were!

ELINOR, EDWARD, LUCY. No one spoke.

MARIANNE. I think, Elinor, we must employ Edward to take care of us in our return to Barton. In a week or two, I suppose, we shall be going.

EDWARD. Edward muttered something,

LUCY. but what it was,

ELINOR. nobody knew,

EDWARD. not even himself.

MARIANNE. Why didn't you come to town sooner Edward?

EDWARD. I was engaged elsewhere.

MARIANNE. Engaged! But what was that, when such friends were to be met?

LUCY. Perhaps, Miss Marianne, you think young men never stand upon engagements, if they have no mind to keep them, little as well as great.

MARIANNE. ...Not so, indeed, not Edward. I believe Edward has the most delicate conscience in the world. He is the most fearful of giving pain, of wounding expectation, and the most incapable of being selfish, of anybody I ever saw.

EDWARD. I...must be going.

MARIANNE. Going so soon! Edward, this must not be.

LUCY. I too must depart. Will you be so good as to escort me out, Mr. Ferrars?

EDWARD. Of course Miss Steele. My apologies Miss Marianne. Miss Dashwood.

(Bow/curtsies. **LUCY** *and* **EDWARD** *exit.)*

MARIANNE. Elinor? How can you...? What can bring Lucy Steele here so often? Could not she see that we wanted her gone!

*(**MARIANNE** exits. **ELINOR** collects herself, whilst the following scene occurs.)*

Scene Seven

(Light special on **JOHN** *and* **FANNY**.*)*

JOHN. They've been in town for quite some time now and people must think it would be proper if the Miss Dashwoods were to stay with us for a while.

FANNY. My love, I would ask them with all my heart, if it was in my power. But I had just settled within myself to ask Miss Lucy Steele to spend a few days with us. I think the attention is due Miss Steele, as her uncle did so very well by Edward.

JOHN. Ah, right! Well, you best invite Miss Steele immediately.

FANNY. Fanny rejoiced in her escape!

> *(JOHN exits, followed by* **FANNY**. *Lights shift back to* **ELINOR** *as* **MRS JENNINGS** *enters.)*

MRS JENNINGS. Lord! my dear Miss Dashwoods! Have you heard the news?

> *(MARIANNE rushes on.)*

ELINOR. No, ma'am. What is it?

MRS JENNINGS. Something so strange! Mr. Edward Ferrars, it seems, has been engaged above this twelvemonth to my cousin Lucy Steele! Yes! That matters should be brought so forward between them, and nobody suspect it?! *I* never happened to see them together, or I am sure *I* should have found it out directly. Well! So this was kept a great secret, for fear of *Mrs*. Ferrars, and neither she nor your brother or sister suspected a word of the matter; till this very morning.

> *(Light special on* **LUCY** *and* **FANNY** *silently acting out the "discovery."* **FANNY** *is not pleased. Lights out.)*

Poor Lucy! They say Mr. Edward is monstrous fond of her—and to have his love used so scornfully! There is no reason on Earth why Mr. Edward and Lucy should not marry; for I am sure Mrs. Ferrars may afford to do very well by her son. If she would only allow him five hundred a-year! Good lord! *Such* a to-do!

(**MRS JENNINGS** *exits.*)

Scene Eight

MARIANNE. How long has this been known to you, Elinor?

ELINOR. When Lucy first came to Barton Park last November, she told me, in confidence, of her engagement.

MARIANNE. *Four* months! Have you known of this *four* months? What! While attending me in all my misery, has this been on your heart? And I have reproached you for being happy! Four months! So calm! so cheerful!

ELINOR. My promise to Lucy, obliged me to be secret. I have very often wished—

MARIANNE. Yet you loved him!

ELINOR. Yes…yes, but after all, Marianne, after all that is bewitching in the idea of a single and constant attachment, of one's happiness depending entirely on one particular person, it is not possible that it should be so. Edward will marry Lucy.

MARIANNE. But he loves *you!* Elinor, if the loss of what is most valued is so easily given up—

ELINOR. For four months, Marianne, I have had all this hanging on my mind, without being at liberty to speak of it to a single creature. It was told me by the very person, whose prior engagement ruined all my hopes; and told me, with triumph. I have had to appear indifferent where I have been most deeply interested. I have had Lucy's hopes and exultation to listen to again and again. I have known myself to be divided from Edward forever and nothing has proved him unworthy nor indifferent to me. My composure has been the effect of constant and painful exertion. If you can think me capable of *ever* feeling—surely you may suppose that I have suffered now.

MARIANNE. Oh Elinor, you have made me hate myself forever.

(**MARIANNE** *weeps*. **ELINOR** *comforts* **MARIANNE**.)

ELINOR. I suppose I must write Mama.

(**MRS JENNINGS** *re-enters.*)

MRS JENNINGS. Well well well! I've just heard! Mr. Edward Ferrars is as honorable as I hoped him to be and refuses to give Lucy up! The poor man is dismissed forever from his mother's home. Mrs. Ferrars has declared she will never see Edward again and has immediately settled her entire estate upon the younger son, Robert Ferrars. Poor Edward! What a gentleman!

(**SERVANT** *enters with letter for* **ELINOR**.)

SERVANT. (*To* **MRS JENNINGS**.) Excuse me Ma'am, Colonel Brandon is here to see you. (*To* **ELINOR**.) A letter for you, Miss.

(**MRS JENNINGS** *and* **SERVANT** *exit*. **MRS DASHWOOD** *enters into light special.*)

ELINOR. It is from Mama!

MRS DASHWOOD. My darling girls...come home! The air, the liberty, the quiet of the country will give you much ease. Elinor, your plan to travel to the Palmers' estate at Cleveland is ideal. Spend the holidays with them and I shall send Thomas to attend you back to Barton.

(*Light special out.* **MRS DASHWOOD** *exits.*)

MARIANNE. Cleveland? No, I cannot. It is too close to // Combe Magna.

ELINOR. Marianne, we will be that much closer to Mama. Cleveland is within a day or two of Barton. We shall remain a week with the Palmers and then continue home.

MARIANNE. Yes...alright. Yes, Elinor, you know best.

(**MARIANNE** *exits.*)

Scene Nine

(Mrs. Jennings' house. **MRS JENNINGS** *leads* **BRANDON** *onstage and quickly exits.)*

MRS JENNINGS. Here she is, Brandon.

BRANDON. Miss Dashwood.

(Bow/curtsy.)

ELINOR. Colonel.

BRANDON. Miss Dashwood, the Palmers have informed me that you are joining our party traveling to their home, Cleveland.

ELINOR. Yes, indeed. I'm pleased to hear you will be among the party.

BRANDON. Thank you, likewise. Miss Dashwood, I have heard of the injustice your friend Mr. Ferrars has suffered from his family. The cruelty, the impolitic cruelty of dividing, or attempting to divide, two young people long attached to each other, is terrible. He and Miss Steele—I understand that he intends to make a career in the Church. Will you be so good as to tell him that the living on my own estate, of Delaford, is now just vacant. I only wish it were more valuable—it is quite a small parsonage.

ELINOR. Oh Colonel, I should think you yourself would want to make such an offer.

BRANDON. All delicacy is required in such a situation and as he is your particular friend... I think it best if it were to come from you.

(As **BRANDON** *exits we transition to the next day as* **EDWARD** *enters.)*

ELINOR. How she should begin—how she should express herself to Edward. To any other person it would have been the easiest thing in the world.

EDWARD. *(Bow/curtsy.)* Miss Dashwood

ELINOR.	EDWARD.
Mr. Ferrars	I'm so sorry!

EDWARD. Excuse me!

ELINOR. No, please—I am charged with a most agreeable office. Colonel Brandon has desired me to say, that understanding you mean to take orders...in the church—he has great pleasure in offering you the living of the parish on his own property which, would enable you to marry—might establish all of your views of happiness.

EDWARD. Colonel Brandon!

ELINOR. Yes. Colonel Brandon means it as a testimony of his concern—for the cruel situation in which your family has placed you—a concern which all your friends, must share *and* as a proof of his high esteem for your behavior on the present occasion.

EDWARD. Colonel Brandon give me a living! Can it be possible?

ELINOR. The unkindness of your own relations has made you astonished to find friendship anywhere.

EDWARD. No, not to find it in you; for I cannot be ignorant that to you, to your goodness, I owe it all. I feel it.

ELINOR. You are very much mistaken. I do assure you that you owe it entirely, to your own merit—your integrity, and Colonel Brandon's discernment of it. I have had no hand in it.

EDWARD. Colonel Brandon seems a man of great worth and respectability.

ELINOR. Indeed, Colonel Brandon is a true gentleman.

EDWARD. I must hurry away then to give *him* those thanks which you will not allow me to give you; to assure him that he has made me a very—an exceedingly happy man.

(Bow/curtsy. **EDWARD** *exits.)*

ELINOR. When I see him again, I shall see him the husband of Lucy Steele.

Scene Ten

(Transition to Cleveland, The Palmers' Estate. **MR PALMER**, **MRS PALMER**, *who is no longer pregnant,* **MRS JENNINGS**, **BRANDON**, *and* **MARIANNE** *enter.)*

MR PALMER. *(Showing the party his estate.)* The Palmers' estate—Cleveland, was a spacious, modern-built house.

MRS PALMER. It has no park, but the pleasure grounds are tolerably extensive.

ELINOR. Nothing was wanting on Mrs. Palmer's side

MRS PALMER. that constant and friendly good humor could do, to make them feel themselves welcome.

ELINOR. The openness of her manner and her kindness were engaging.

MRS PALMER. Her folly, though evident

ELINOR. was not disgusting,

MRS PALMER. as it was not conceited!

ELINOR. Elinor could have forgiven everything

*(***MRS PALMER*** laughs.)*

but her laugh. Elinor even found Mr. Palmer

MR PALMER. perfectly the gentleman in his behavior to all his visitors.

MARIANNE. Marianne was full of emotion from the consciousness of being only thirty miles from Combe Magna. I must be outside!

*(Light special on **MARIANNE**.)*

She stole away through the winding shrubberies to gain that view where, her eye could fondly rest on the farthest ridge of hills in the horizon. Combe Magna. Willoughby. She resolved to spend almost every hour of every day while she remained with the Palmers, in the indulgence of such solitary rambles.

Scene Eleven

(Lights special out as **MARIANNE** *returns to "the house."* **MARIANNE** *sneezes.)*

BRANDON. Bless you, Miss Marianne.

*(***BRANDON*** gives* **MARIANNE** *his handkerchief.)*

Are you quite well?

MARIANNE. Oh yes, thank you Colonel.

BRANDON. After two twilight walks later in the week,

MARIANNE. all *over* the distant grounds,

ELINOR. Assisted by the still greater imprudence of sitting in her wet shoes and stockings

MARIANNE. Marianne developed a violent cold.

ELINOR. Mr. Palmer…would you be so kind as to call for your apothecary? To bed, my darling.

(Transition to the "bedroom." **ELINOR** *puts* **MARIANNE** *to bed. The rest of the group observe from outside the bedroom.)*

MRS PALMER. Oh, yes! A good night's rest will cure her entirely!

ELINOR. A very restless night, however, awaited them.

*(***APOTHECARY*** enters to examine* **MARIANNE.***)*

MARIANNE. Marianne was so very feverish with a pain in her limbs,

APOTHECARY. *and* a cough, *and* a sore throat. She needs rest as her fever is very severe. Her disorder seems to have a putrid tendency that might without care and luck bring an infection.

MRS PALMER. My baby! The baby!

MR PALMER. Thus followed the Palmers' immediate removal…to the home of a nearby relation. *(To* **ELINOR.***)* If you need anything…please send for me. We are not far. Brandon.

MRS JENNINGS. *(Exiting.)* Poor Miss Marianne…

(The **PALMERS** *and* **MRS JENNINGS** *exit.* **ELINOR**
nurses **MARIANNE** *whilst* **BRANDON** *paces*
upstage.)

ELINOR. restless and uncomfortable. Marianne slept all day
in near delirium...

MARIANNE. *(Starting awake.)* Is Mama coming?

ELINOR. ...Mama, coming here? Uh...

MARIANNE. She must not go round by London. I shall
never see her, if she goes by London.

ELINOR. Marianne's pulse was lower and quicker than ever!

MARIANNE. Mama! She told me... *(Mumbles feverishly.)*

*(***FEMALE SERVANT** *enters with a bowl of small
towels.* **BRANDON** *takes them and delivers them to*
ELINOR.*)*

BRANDON. Please...let me do something.

ELINOR. My mother—it would be a great comfort to have
my mother here.

BRANDON. Of course—

*(***BRANDON** *rushes off.* **ELINOR** *steps back to*
MARIANNE. SERVANT *assists.)*

MARIANNE. Mama... Mama...

ELINOR. It was *another* long night of almost equal suffering
to both. Hour after hour passed away in sleepless pain
and delirium on Marianne's side and in the most cruel
anxiety on Elinor's. Her fever is unabated...almost
three days and she remains in this heavy stupor. It must
break. The fever must break.

SERVANT. Yes, Miss

ELINOR. Elinor had no sense of fatigue, no capability of
sleep about her.

SERVANT. The young miss scarcely stirred from her sister's
bed.

*(***MARIANNE** *slowly begins to sleep restfully.)*

ELINOR. I think…wait… I must examine again. No, I am
  right. Her pulse is stronger.

SERVANT. Half an hour passed away,

> *(After a tense moment* **MARIANNE** *opens her eyes
> and smiles weakly.)*

MARIANNE. Elinor…

> *(***ELINOR** *hugs and kisses* **MARIANNE**—*sounds of
> a doorbell.)*

ELINOR. Oh! One moment my darling. Rest.

> *(Lights shift as* **SERVANT** *helps* **MARIANNE** *exit.)*

Scene Twelve

(Transition to Cleveland, Drawing Room.)

ELINOR. Elinor rushed to the drawing-room. Mama!

*(***WILLOUGHBY** *enters.)*

ELINOR. Willoughby!

*(***ELINOR** *stops then turns to go.)*

WILLOUGHBY. Miss Dashwood, I entreat you to stay.

ELINOR. No, sir, I shall *not* stay. Your business cannot be with *me*. Mr. Palmer is—

WILLOUGHBY. Is your sister out of danger? I heard it from the servant. Is it true? Is it really true? For God's sake tell me, is she out of danger, or is she not?

ELINOR. We hope she is.

WILLOUGHBY. When Sir John told me yesterday that Marianne was dying—

ELINOR. Mr. Willoughby, I am not at leisure to remain with you longer.

WILLOUGHBY. I've come all the way from London.

ELINOR. What is it that you mean by it?

WILLOUGHBY. I mean to…offer some kind of explanation, some kind of apology, to obtain something like forgiveness from Mari—from your sister. Please! *(Beat.)* When I first became intimate with your family, I had no other intention, than to pass the time pleasantly. Your sister's lovely person—and her behavior to me, was of a kind—But at first I must confess, thinking only of my own amusement, I endeavored, to make myself pleasing to her, without any design of returning her affection.

ELINOR. Do not—

WILLOUGHBY. I insist! Miss Dashwood, my fortune was never large, and I have always spent beyond—every year added to my debts. My aunt's death was to set me free; yet that event was possibly far distant. I *had* to marry a woman of fortune, thus, to attach myself to your sister was not a thing to be considered. Yet with a selfishness, a cruelty—I was trying to engage her regard without a thought of returning it. But I did not *THEN* know what it was to love. To have resisted such attractions, to have withstood such tenderness! The happiest hours of my life were what I spent with her… and I had determined to ask her to be my wife—but a circumstance occurred—an unlucky circumstance.

ELINOR. I have heard it all.

WILLOUGHBY. Ah, of course…our good friend the Colonel. Could his account be an impartial one? I do not mean to justify myself but do not suppose that because Miss Betsy Williams was injured she was irreproachable and because I was a libertine, she must be a saint! I do not mean, however, to defend myself. *(Beat.)* When my aunt was apprised of this news, I was dismissed from her favor and her house.

ELINOR. And this is all, Sir?

WILLOUGHBY. All? No, then to learn that Marianne had come to London! If you *can* pity me, Miss Dashwood— with my head and heart full of your sister, I was forced to play the happy lover to another woman!

ELINOR. Your *own* letter to Marianne; so cruel! What have you to say about that?

WILLOUGHBY. My wife intercepted the last letter your sister sent me and it made her more jealous than ever. What do you think of my wife's style of letter writing?

ELINOR. Your wife? But it was your handwriting!

WILLOUGHBY. She dictated such sentences as I was ashamed to put my name to…but I needed her money. My *business* was to declare myself a scoundrel. I copied my wife's words, and parted with the last relics of Marianne. I was forced to put them up, and could not even kiss them—the dear lock of hair—

ELINOR. You ought not to speak this way. You have made your own choice. It was not forced on you.

WILLOUGHBY. Yes, but you see, my intentions were not always wrong. Have I explained away any part of my guilt?

ELINOR. The misery that you have inflicted—

WILLOUGHBY. Will you repeat to your sister what I have been telling you? Tell her of *my* misery—tell her that my heart was never inconstant to her, and if you will, that at this moment she is dearer to me than ever.

ELINOR. Sir—

WILLOUGHBY. Please! …Please. God Bless you.

ELINOR. And with these words, he ran out of the room!

> (**WILLOUGHBY** *exits. A beat.* **MRS DASHWOOD** *enters.* **BRANDON** *and* **MARGARET** *behind her.*)

ELINOR. Mama! Mama. She is safe. The fever is broke.

> (**MARIANNE** *enters with help from the* **SERVANT**.)

MARIANNE. Mama?

MRS DASHWOOD. My darling Marianne…

MARIANNE. Thank you… Colonel Brandon. Mama, I want to go home…to Barton.

Scene Thirteen

(Transition to Barton Cottage. All exit except **MARIANNE** *and* **ELINOR***, walking through the hills.)*

ELINOR. As Marianne recovered, Elinor began to see in her

MARIANNE. a composure of mind

ELINOR. which she trusted to be the result of serious reflection. It must eventually lead Marianne to contentment and cheerfulness. And Elinor, therefore, feared recounting Willoughby's visit as it might again unsettle her sister's mind.

MARIANNE. I'd forgotten how beautiful and lush it is here at Barton. How ideal. How picturesque.

(The sisters walk arm in arm.)

When the weather is settled, we will take long walks together every day. Elinor, I know we shall be happy. *(Beat.)* There, exactly there…there I fell; and there I first saw Willoughby. Oh… I am thankful I can look with so little pain on the spot. To say that I shall soon or that I shall *ever* forget him, would be idle. But as for regret, I have done with that… If I could be allowed to think that he was not always acting a part, not always deceiving me. Not so very wicked…

ELINOR. If you could be assured of that, you think you should be easy?

MARIANNE. Yes, for it is horrible to suspect him of such designs and what must it make me appear to myself but shamefully unguarded. I wish his secret reflections may be no more unpleasant than my own. He will suffer enough in them.

ELINOR. Do you compare your conduct with *his*?

MARIANNE. No. I compare it with what it ought to have been; I compare it with yours. I see in my past behavior, nothing but a series of imprudence towards myself, and want of kindness to others. I see that my own feelings *prepared* my sufferings and almost led me to the grave. Had I died! In what misery should I have left you, my nurse, my friend, my sister! You—you above all, have been wronged by me.

ELINOR. Marianne—

MARIANNE. I, and only I, knew your heart and its sorrows; yet to what did it influence me? Not to any compassion that could benefit you or myself. No, the future must be my proof! My feelings shall be governed and my temper improved. If I could but know *HIS* heart, everything would become easy.

ELINOR. Elinor heard this and soon found herself leading to the fact—the description of Willoughby's visit at Cleveland: his apology, his repentance, and his continued regard.

(Beat. The girls embrace.)

Scene Fourteen

(Transition to Barton Cottage. **MRS DASHWOOD**, **MARGARET**, *and* **THOMAS** *enter. Ladies are reading, drawing, etc.)*

MRS DASHWOOD. I was pleased to see Colonel Brandon yesterday...such an intelligent, kind gentleman.

MARGARET. I like him very much.

MARIANNE. Yes.

THOMAS. Oh, I suppose you know, ma'am, that Mr. Ferrars is married.

(Beat.)

MRS DASHWOOD. Who told you that Mr. Ferrars was married, Thomas?

THOMAS. I see Mr. Ferrars myself, ma'am, this morning in Exeter, and his lady too, Miss Steele as was. She inquired after you, ma'am, and the young ladies, and bid me I should give her compliments and Mr. Ferrars'. She was always a very affable young lady so I made free to wish her joy.

MRS DASHWOOD. Thank you Thomas.

*(***THOMAS** *exits, going about his work.* **MARGARET** *follows him.)*

MRS DASHWOOD. Mrs. Dashwood suddenly feared that she had been unjust, inattentive, nay, almost unkind, to her Elinor; —that Marianne's affliction had too much engrossed her tenderness, and led her to forget that in Elinor she might have a daughter suffering almost as much.

ELINOR. Elinor now found the difference between the expectation of an unpleasant event, and certainty itself.

*(***MARGARET** *runs back on.)*

MARGARET. Someone is approaching...on horseback!

(They all move to the window.)

MARIANNE. It is Colonel Brandon! *(***MARIANNE** *still has his handkerchief.)*

MARGARET. I don't think so. I think—

ELINOR. *(Realizing who it is.)* I WILL be calm.

MARGARET. it is Edward!

> *(The* **DASHWOOD LADIES** *pretend to be busy.* **THOMAS** *shows in* **EDWARD.***)*

THOMAS. Mr. Ferrars.

MRS DASHWOOD. Edward…how wonderful. May I wish you joy!

EDWARD. Edward stammered out an unintelligible reply.

ELINOR. Was the weather pleasant on your journey, Mr. Ferrars? It has been quite dry here.

EDWARD. Uh, yes it was…very dry.

MARIANNE. Marianne retreated as much as possible out of sight, to conceal her distress.

MRS DASHWOOD. I hope you left *Mrs.* Ferrars very well, Edward.

EDWARD. …Yes.

MRS DASHWOOD. Is Mrs. Ferrars at Exeter?

EDWARD. At Exeter? No, my mother is in town.

MRS DASHWOOD. I meant to inquire for Mrs. Edward Ferrars.

ELINOR. Elinor dared not look up;

MRS DASHWOOD. but her mother

MARIANNE. and Marianne both kept their eyes on Edward.

EDWARD. Perhaps you mean—my brother—you mean Mrs.—Mrs. Robert Ferrars.

MARIANNE. Mrs. Robert Ferrars!

EDWARD. Perhaps you do not know—you may not have heard that my *brother* is lately married to Miss Lucy Steele.

MARIANNE. Your…brother…is…

MRS DASHWOOD. Your *brother*…

EDWARD. Yes, they were married last week. Apparently, they were much thrown together after I left town and… Miss Steele, I should say, Mrs. Robert Ferrars released me from our…from our engagement soon after.

MARIANNE. Lucy Steele married your brother?

ELINOR. Elinor could sit it no longer.

> (**ELINOR** *crosses away and bursts into tears. A private moment as* **EDWARD** *follows* **ELINOR**.)

EDWARD. Edward's reason for traveling to Barton, was only…to ask Elinor to marry him. In what manner he expressed himself,

ELINOR. and how he was received, need not be particularly told.

EDWARD. This only need be said—that when they all sat down to table about three hours after his arrival,

ELINOR. Edward had secured his lady, engaged her mother's consent,

> (**ELINOR** *and* **EDWARD** *rejoin the others.*)

EDWARD. and was not only in the rapturous profession of the lover, but, in the reality of reason and truth, one of the happiest of men.

MRS DASHWOOD. Mrs. Dashwood, was too happy to be comfortable and knew not how to love Edward, nor praise Elinor enough,

MARIANNE. Marianne could speak *her* happiness only by tears.

MARGARET. Hurrah! I knew it! I knew it!

ELINOR. But Elinor—how are *her* feelings to be described? She was oppressed. She was overcome by her own felicity.

> (*Light special on* **ELINOR** *and* **EDWARD**. *All others remain onstage.*)

EDWARD. Miss Steele…was a foolish, idle inclination on my side. The consequence of ignorance of the world and want of employment.

ELINOR. *(Smiling.)* Well, as an engaged man, your behavior at Norland was certainly very wrong.

EDWARD. I...felt that I...admired you but told myself it was only friendship. I fooled only myself.

ELINOR. And what of your brother and Miss Steele?! That is...a puzzle.

EDWARD. I imagine the vanity of the one was worked on by the flattery of the other.

(**ELINOR** *laughs.*)

Can you forgive me, my darling Elinor?

ELINOR. Forgiven... Edward.

(**EDWARD** *kisses* **ELINOR'S** *hand. Light special out.*)

Scene Fifteen

(Barton Cottage. Several Days Later. The **DASHWOOD FAMILY** *and* **EDWARD** *are all happily engaged in activity.* **BRANDON** *and* **THOMAS** *enter.)*

THOMAS. Colonel Brandon.

MARIANNE. Colonel Brandon!

BRANDON. Good Day! Miss Marianne, I've brought you those books.

MARIANNE. Oh, how thoughtful.

*(**MARIANNE** and **BRANDON** look at books while* **MRS DASHWOOD** *joins* **ELINOR** *and* **EDWARD**.)

MRS DASHWOOD. My partiality does not blind me; Colonel Brandon certainly is not so handsome as Willoughby—but at the same time, there is something much more pleasing in his countenance. There was always a something, if you remember, in Willoughby's eyes at times, which I did not like.

ELINOR. Elinor could not remember that.

MRS DASHWOOD. And his manners, the Colonel's manners are more pleasing to me than Willoughby's ever were. Their gentleness, their attention to others, and their unstudied simplicity is much more accordant with Marianne's real disposition.

ELINOR. With such a confederacy against her—

MARIANNE. with a knowledge so intimate of Colonel Brandon's goodness and with a conviction of his fond attachment to herself—

BRANDON. What could she do? *(**BRANDON** kneels.)*

MRS DASHWOOD. Marianne Dashwood was born to an extraordinary fate.

ELINOR. She was born to discover the falsehood of her own opinions and to counteract, by her conduct, her most favorite maxims.

MARIANNE. She was born to *overcome* a first passion…and with no sentiment superior to strong esteem and lively friendship, voluntarily to give her hand to another.

(**MARIANNE** *does.* **BRANDON** *stands.*)

BRANDON. But Marianne could never love by halves

MARIANNE. And her whole heart became, in time, passionately devoted to her husband.

BRANDON. "One hour with thee! When sun is set,

Oh, what can teach me to forget"

BRANDON & MARIANNE. "The thankless labors of the day;

The hopes, the wishes, flung away;"

ELINOR & MARIANNE. "The increasing wants, and lessening gains,

The master's pride, who scorns my pains?"

ELINOR. One hour with thee.

(Couples kiss! Then **ELINOR** *and* **MARIANNE** *embrace. Lights out.)*

The End

Jen Taylor first read *Pride and Prejudice* when she was eight years old, and she couldn't fathom why Elizabeth Bennet would choose the haughty Darcy over the kind, charming Wickham. In any case, she was an immediate Austen fan and, thankfully, her discernment developed with age. Jen is honored to help bring Austen's novels to life with Book-It Repertory Theatre. In addition to *Sense and Sensibility* she co-adapted *Persuasion,* and has thrice played the role of Elizabeth Bennet in Book-It's *Pride and Prejudice.* Jen is also an accomplished actor, having performed at major theatres across the Northwest, and works extensively as a voice actor in radio, television, audiobooks and video games.

Book-It Repertory Theatre began in Seattle, Washington in 1990 as a company of actors who believed that everyone has the right to read. Today, Book-It is a vibrant, nationally known theatre company that transforms great works of classic and contemporary literature into exciting fully staged works for audiences young and old. With more than 100 world-premiere adaptations to its credit—many of which have garnered rave reviews and gone on to subsequent productions all over the country–Book-It is widely respected for the consistent artistic excellence of its work. Book-It's combined programs ignite the imaginations of more than 70,000 people a year through the power of live theatre. The company's honors include a 2010 Seattle Mayor's Arts Award, a Paul G. Allen Family Foundation Founder's Award, a 2012 Washington Governor's Arts Award, and three Gregory Awards for Outstanding Production. www.book-it.org